W9-CAM-528

Also by Allison Gutknecht

Spring Break Mistake

The Bling Queen

Pizza Is the Best Breakfast
(And Other Lessons I've Learned)

Never Wear Red Lipstick on Picture Day
(And Other Lessons I've Learned)

A Cast Is the Perfect Accessory
(And Other Lessons I've Learned)

Don't Wear Polka-Dot Underwear with White Pants
(And Other Lessons I've Learned)

SING LIKE NOBODY'S LISTENING

Allison Gutknecht

ALADDIN

New York   London   Toronto   Sydney   New Delhi

ALADDIN
An imprint of Simon & Schuster Children's Publishing Division
1230 Avenue of the Americas, New York, New York 10020
First Aladdin hardcover edition January 2018
Text copyright © 2018 by Allison Gutknecht
Jacket illustration copyright © 2018 by Lucy Truman
Also available in an Aladdin M!X paperback edition.
For information about special discounts for bulk purchases, please contact Simon & Schuster Special Sales at 1-866-506-1949 or business@simonandschuster.com.
The Simon & Schuster Speakers Bureau can bring authors to your live event. For more information or to book an event contact the Simon & Schuster Speakers Bureau at 1-866-248-3049 or visit our website at www.simonspeakers.com.
Jacket designed by Jessica Handelman
Interior designed by Heather Palisi
The text of this book was set in Apollo.
Manufactured in the United States of America 1217 FFG
2 4 6 8 10 9 7 5 3 1
Library of Congress Control Number 2017957606
ISBN 978-1-4814-7157-2 (hc)
ISBN 978-1-4814-7156-5 (pbk)
ISBN 978-1-4814-7158-9 (eBook)

For the Loop,
the group who has always marched together,
if never quite in step

★ 1 ★

The last time I rolled my eyes this high, I'm pretty sure I caught a glimpse of Mars.

Mom always tells me that if I keep rolling my eyes like this, they're going to get stuck in the corners of my sockets. But sometimes, a solid eye roll is the only way to respond to something so ridiculous that words could never suffice.

Something like Jada's current all-out, drop-down battle with Mason Swenson, her self-declared personal nemesis.

"I know you did that on purpose!" she yells at him, smack in the middle of the seventh-grade wing.

"Of course I did it on purpose," Mason counters, looking pleased with himself. "Do you think anyone has ever tied a locker closed with dental floss *by accident*?"

I twist my own combination and throw open the door with a flourish, letting the metal bang triumphantly. I unzip my bag and retrieve my latest clipping of Colby Cash—this one from an advertisement for his new show, *Non-Instrumental*—and I add it to the collage of his head shots decorating the interior of my locker. We're forbidden to use Scotch tape for such trimmings, but no one in administration has said anything about star stickers, which is what I affix to the four corners of Colby's picture. The stickers are more fitting anyway, since Colby Cash is the biggest star in the universe.

Or at least, he's the biggest star in *my* universe.

I run my finger along the seam of the photo, smoothing it with a smile, and trying my best to block out the feud going on beside me. But Jada has worked herself into such a frenzy—one dramatic even by her standards—that there's no escaping her screeches. "You're so rude!" she scoffs, pulling at the strings of floss that Mason has methodically tied from the lever of her locker to the hook inside his own. This means that whenever Jada tries to open hers, the strands tighten into a taut line, nearly impossible to break bare handed.

"Why don't you ask Mrs. Nieska for a pair of scissors and cut it open?" I suggest. "So that we can all move on with our lives."

"No, you know what? 'Rude' isn't good enough a word for you," Jada continues her rant toward Mason, ignoring me. "You are vile." She nearly spits the word at him, which only seems to give Mason more satisfaction. While they continue their tiff, I walk down the hall to Mrs. Nieska's room and head straight to her desk.

"Good afternoon, Wylie," Mrs. Nieska says, glancing up. Her glasses sit at their usual perch on the very tip of her nose, and it is a wonder of physics that they don't constantly slip onto her chin.

"Good afternoon," I echo. "May I please borrow your scissors?" Mrs. Nieska begins rustling in her desk drawer until she locates a pair, and she hands them to me without asking a single *why?*

And this is exactly the reason Mrs. Nieska is the Willow Oak Middle School teacher from whom to request such favors. She's not one to ask questions when she doesn't care about the answers.

"Thanks, be right back!" I chirp, skipping out the door and back to Jada, gripping the blades firmly. As I approach, I discover that not only has Jada still not managed to pry open her locker, but she also hasn't taken the advice that I am constantly giving her: Just ignore Mason.

"Yeah, well, you have two 'sons' in your name," I hear her retaliate, and though I *am* her best friend, even I have to admit that this is not her greatest comeback.

"MaSON SwenSON," Jada continues, insistent that she's going to make this into a good point. "It's redundant."

"Even for you, that's lame," Mason says, smirking as he crosses his arms, casually leaning against the offending locker, his baseball cap—which he's not supposed to be wearing in school, I might add—cocked at a backward angle on his head. I step in between them, and in a single snip, free Jada's locker.

"There. Now can we *please* go to lunch before I faint from hunger?" I turn on my heel and head back to Mrs.

Nieska's room, placing the scissors on her desk. "Thank you!" I call, and Mrs. Nieska gives me a thumbs-up, not taking her eyes off grading the latest round of pre-algebra quizzes.

I sweep my eyes back and forth across the hallway, searching for Jada, but she and Mason have both (finally) abandoned our locker bank, and I assume she has headed to the cafeteria. I walk toward the large wooden doors and open them with my hip, then I head to the third table on the left, all the way against the wall. Sure enough, she's stationed in our designated spot, poking at her phone with her eyebrows pointed down. Two faint lines are in the center of her brow—the ones that appear when she is at her most frustrated—and they look especially deep at the moment.

I plop my bagged lunch on the table and step over the bench to sit. "Can we please not spend the entire period discussing Mason?" I decide to cut off her tirade before it can begin.

"He is the worst," she proclaims like there's an exclamation point after each word, her dark eyes shiny with fury.

"Yes, yes, I know. So let's not waste any more time on

him," I say. "Not when Colby's premiere is right around the corner and we can talk about *that*."

Jada examines her phone screen like it's offending her before tossing it in her bag. "Which night is this show on again?" she asks.

"Monday. Come over at least fifteen minutes early so we can get our snacks assembled. I don't want any distractions during the show itself."

"That's why a nifty thing called the pause button was invented," Jada teases me, beginning to pile potato chips in between the layers of her sandwich.

"No, we have to watch him live," I explain. "That's the whole point. So we can follow along with his online posts at the same time."

"Whatever you say, Mrs. Cash," Jada says as a chip crumb flies from her mouth.

"Thanks for that," I say, wiping my cheek. "Aren't you excited to see Colby back on TV? It will be like old times."

"I guess," Jada says distractedly, half her face now hidden behind her hair, which is even darker than her eyes and falls in long waves like black licorice. "But it hasn't been the same since Marquis Machine broke up. I still have trouble seeing him as a stand-alone singer."

"Bite your tongue. He's awesome. And plus, he's hosting this show, not singing. Though I hope they let him sing once in a while. Like every single week. For the whole hour."

"You should be his publicist," Jada tells me, and I give her a serious nod. Jada and I had become fans of Colby Cash in elementary school, when he played keyboard in the boy group Marquis Machine. Our love of the band, even then, bordered on over-the-top, though Colby was always our favorite member. We even created our own Colby Cash scrapbook, where we preserved our acquired Colby-related memorabilia, along with our personal poetic tributes to his amber-hued eyes and thick crop of auburn hair. But nearly a year ago, soon after we started middle school, Marquis Machine broke up, and Colby struck out as a solo performer. For the past few months he's been relatively out of the limelight, until he was named host of the latest season of *Non-Instrumental*: a TV competition show featuring a cappella groups. And I couldn't wait to have Colby in my living room every week, no matter what the context.

"Remind me to add more pages to the back of our scrapbook," I tell Jada. "I'm sure we'll have new stuff to include."

"So you're really going to fall down the Colby Cash rabbit hole again?" she asks.

"What do you mean?"

Jada shrugs. "I don't know. I feel like we left our love of Colby behind in fifth grade."

"Um, have you seen my locker?"

"Wylie. Everyone has seen your locker. People in space can see your locker," Jada says with a smirk, and I mime throwing a carrot stick at her. "But we're in seventh grade now. Don't you think we should be doing different things than we did when we were younger? This is our middle school experience!" She gestures wildly around the room like she's the star of a junior high infomercial.

I run my fingers through my chestnut-brown bangs, which tickle the tops of my eyelashes, and I push them back into my hair while considering this. "You haven't given up fighting with Mason," I point out. "And you've been doing that forever."

"I would if he would stop torturing me," Jada insists. "But seriously, it's the start of a brand-new year—maybe it's time we tried something else."

"Something like what?" I ask. But before Jada can answer, the room suddenly erupts in a chorus of whoops and cheers, originating at the table where the soccer teams sit. Every day, the boys try to build a skyscraper out of trash, and today's has managed to tower above the heads of even the tallest on the squad. The players high-five and congratulate themselves before an aide forces them to disassemble their structure, resulting in many boos.

I glance around at the other tables watching them— there are the sports teams: the runners, the baseball and softball players, the tennis players, the bowlers (yes, we have a bowling team); the robotics team sits with the math Olympiad and the debate team eats next to the science troop; there are two tables of band members, a separate one for the orchestra, and a whole corner dedicated to the theatre people. The day we started sixth grade, these factions seemed to form automatically, leaving the rest of us behind. And sometimes I wonder what it's like to sit at one of those tables, to have a seemingly endless supply of friends, of people to fill your lunch conversation, or to gather around your locker in the morning, so many deep that they block half the hallway.

"Break?" Jada asks, halting my thoughts. She holds a large chocolate chip cookie across the table, waiting for me to reach out and snap it in half so we can share.

Once I do so, we "clink" the two sides together, as if raising a silent toast, and then we each take a bite.

And as curious as I am about those other tables, I'm still okay at mine. After all, if there are only two of you, you're always guaranteed at least half the cookie.

★ 2 ★

Jada and I trudge home after school through the same development we've lived in our whole lives, the sights as familiar as the walls of our own bedrooms.

"I need to get him back," Jada announces. This afternoon, Mason topped his dental floss stunt with a bouquet of confetti, which he dumped through the slits of Jada's locker, leaving a heap of hole-punched dots scattered over her belongings.

"I don't know why you let him get to you," I say,

stepping to the side to crunch on an especially inviting leaf. "If you would ignore him, like I always—"

"There's no ignoring Mason," Jada interrupts me. "It's like his personal goal in life is to annoy me."

"Because you let him! You react too strongly. It only eggs him on."

"I wish my parents would move. I can't take knowing he's next door spying on me."

"So you'd move away from *me* in order to avoid Mason?" I ask, placing my hand near my heart with exaggerated hurt.

"Not out of Willow Oak entirely, but to another part of town," Jada explains. "Or actually, he should move. He's the one who started this."

I roll my eyes, but Jada is too busy grimacing to notice. The most absurd part of this feud is that it started way back in preschool—before I even knew Jada—when Jada's mom sent her to Mason's house to play. Mason's family had a giant seesaw in their backyard—a wooden one with animal faces that you held on to as you rose up and down.

Or didn't rise up and down, as this particular case may be.

It seems that at this playdate, Mason, who was quite

an expert at his seesaw, convinced Jada to board the other side, and once she was high in the air, he sat stubbornly on the ground, refusing to lower her down. Jada swears this lasted at least fifteen minutes, though considering we didn't know how to tell time yet, it was probably much less. Once Jada was good and upset—"Tears and everything!"—Mason finally pushed his way up in the air, sending Jada crashing onto the mulch below. The force caused her to roll off her seat, and though she was essentially fine—"I got a splinter!"—she's never been able to let it go.

And Mason has presumably never been able to let go of the part where Jada marched in the back door of his house and immediately—and theatrically—tattled on him to his mom.

I've never known Jada and Mason to get along, and it's not like I expected them to make peace. But at this point, it seems crazy that they're continuing to argue like tantruming toddlers—one would think they could at least be civil.

"What are you guys doing later?" I ask, attempting to change the subject. "The usual Friday pizza and game night?"

"Ugh, yes," Jada answers. "I guarantee that by six

thirty, the boys will be wrestling on the floor over who gets to be the green marker on the *Sorry!* board."

I laugh. Jada's house, with her two younger brothers barreling around, is always ten times noisier than mine. "I think it's fun. More exciting than playing games with two people."

"Like I always tell you, you're welcome to join us."

"I know, but then I'd be leaving my mom," I say with a shrug. "And since I have to go to my dad's tomorrow . . ." I trail off.

"She could come too," Jada says as we approach the fork in the sidewalk where we part. "You know that, right?"

"I do. Thanks."

"Have fun at your dad's," she calls in a singsong voice.

"Yeah, right," I snort as she walks away. "Text me for entertainment, please."

"Wish me luck making it home without running into Mason!"

"If you see him, turn around and come to my house," I tell her. "Or better yet—*just ignore him.*"

"Yeah, yeah. See you," Jada says, waving good-bye. As I round the corner, a harsh wind hits me head-on, raising chilled goose bumps up and down my arms.

"Smells like snow, don't you think?" I hear behind me.

"You're back al—?" I turn, expecting to find Jada. Instead, I see Libby running to catch me, the blond tail of her braid bouncing on her back.

"That would be amazing if it did," I say. "But it seems like wishful thinking."

"A girl can dream." Libby falls in stride beside me.

"Whoa, your hair," I say, stopping so I can admire her creation. "You did it inside out." Libby wears a French braid every single day, which seems a little babyish now that she's in sixth grade, but she's too sweet for me to ever tell her that.

"Yep. Variety is the spice of life, as my grandmother would say," she remarks. "It's not that hard—you just tuck the hair under instead of over."

"I can barely make a regular braid, let alone a French one."

"It was either learn or let my dad do it," Libby says. "And he still hasn't mastered a ponytail. For most of first grade, I looked like the Bride of Frankenstein."

I smile. "You're not going to your grandmother's today?" Libby's mom passed away when she was very young, so she spends almost as much time at her grandmother's house as she does at her own. Between her visits there and my trips to Dad's, I hardly see her, despite the fact that she lives next door.

Libby shakes her head. "I convinced my dad to let me come home on my own a few days a week. In fact, I convinced him of this by pointing out that *you* started coming home alone when you were in sixth grade. So thanks—that definitely sweetened the pot."

"You're welcome." We turn down our respective driveways, which are separated by a slim sliver of grass. "What are you up to this weekend?"

She hops from one foot to the other, energy evaporating through her pores. "I have a mosaic to finish. I'm redoing my grandmother's mailbox."

"A mosaic?" Libby has always been artistic, evidenced by the weekly rotation of homemade wreaths and wind catchers framing her front stoop, but I had never seen her create something as complicated as a mosaic.

"Yep. Dad buys me cheap plates at the discount store, and I shatter them in the basement and then glue the pieces together in different designs," she explains. "It's superfun, if you ever need to get some frustrations out."

I laugh. "I'll keep that in mind. And if you need a

rest from hurling plates, I'm sure my mom is cooking something odd for dinner tonight."

"Awesome!" Libby chirps. "But we're supposed to be heading to my grandmother's. That's why I need to finish her mailbox in two shakes of a lamb's tail."

"Good luck," I call after her as she skips toward her porch. Sometimes I wonder if Libby and I would be better friends if she weren't a year behind me in school, if seeing each other on a regular basis would translate to a deeper connection. But no matter what, as far as next-door neighbors go, I had definitely won the lottery compared to Jada. After all, Libby Soleil has never knocked me off a seesaw.

When I walk in, Mom is banging through the kitchen in her typical day-off outfit: sweatpants that look twenty years old, a slightly grimy T-shirt, and a mismatched floral scarf.

"What are you making?" I ask as she kisses me on the cheek in greeting.

"I found a new chili recipe," she answers. "I thought I'd give it a whirl." Mom loves to cook, and she's always making something new. Last Friday, it was stuffed peppers, the week prior was grilled tofu, and before that, her take on beef Wellington. (I call it "her take" because no one who has ever worked in a kitchen would consider it anything resembling "Wellington.") Even if they're a little "off," most of Mom's creations taste good. But sometimes, I long for the traditions of a house like Jada's, where every Friday night means pizza and board games instead of a grab-bag production from the crisper drawer.

I deposit my bag on the floor and pull myself onto a counter stool. "How was school?" Mom asks as she stirs the steaming pot on the stove.

"Fine. Mason tied Jada's locker closed with floss and then sprinkled it with confetti, so of course, she flipped out."

"That boy is a piece of work," Mom says, shaking her head.

"I keep telling her to ignore him, but she never listens."

"Part of her probably enjoys the attention, despite how much she complains about it," Mom says. "You know Jada has always thrived on an opportunity to be dramatic."

"That's very true," I say, pushing my bangs back through my hair.

"I wish you would let me trim those," Mom says. "You'd be a lot more comfortable if they weren't tickling your lashes all the time." I roll my eyes at this, purposely doing so when Mom isn't facing me so she can't say they're going to get stuck up there. But before I can defend my hairstyle, my phone buzzes with a text from Dad—the same one he sends every Friday night when he's scheduled to pick me up the next day.

See you tomorrow morning at 8:00, Wylie! We're all looking forward to it.

I sigh. See you then, I write back, purposely not including an exclamation mark or a smiley face or anything that would convey excitement.

"Who was that?" Mom asks.

"Dad," I answer curtly. "Reminding me of my pickup time. As if it ever changes."

Mom begins ladling the chili out of the pot. "It's only one day, Wy. You can make it through one day."

"Just because I can doesn't mean I want to," I say, rising from the stool and lifting my bag from the floor. "I'm going to pack." I retreat to my room and pull my patchwork bag out of the closet. I throw in a pair of pajamas, a toothbrush, a sweatshirt, and a magazine featuring an article on Colby which I've only read once so far. Even though Dad tells me I'm welcome to leave items at his house, I prefer taking them back and forth as if I'm staying overnight at a hotel, at a location that I'm only visiting.

At a place that will never be home.

★ 3 ★

I can't wait until we can drive so I can get myself away from here, I text Jada the following afternoon while huddled on Dad's couch. I stare at the phone, willing her to respond, as Asher and Amelia leap around in front of me, their latest video game blaring from the speakers.

This is the problem with Dad's house—well, one of many problems, but this is a big one: I have no place to myself. At my house, Mom and I have more space than we need. It's not that we live in a mansion, but at the very least, I have my own room. Here, I sleep on a trundle that gets pulled out from under Amelia's bed for the every other Saturday I visit. But even though my trundle resides there, hers is definitely not *my* room. Because any time I so much as step foot over the threshold, Amelia is on my heels, padding through the upstairs in bare feet while decked out in a rotating supply of princess dresses. And I make a point to stay as far from Asher's room as possible, since it smells like a deadly combination of grass stains and stale cheese curls. Which officially leaves me nowhere to hide.

Coming to Dad's house was one thing six years ago, before Asher was born. When it was only Dad and his wife, Amy, our weekends together were nice, calm, even fun. But then Asher came along, and then Amelia two years later, and with each month that passed, it felt more and more like I was an intruder in another family's life rather than a member of my own. It's not that Dad and Amy aren't still nice to me—it's that they're *too* nice. Like they're putting on their best selves in an effort to make me feel welcome. And the more stops they pull out in an attempt to please me, the more I feel like retreating.

"Remember—the winner of this game takes on Wylie

next," Dad says as he passes through the room. The two terrors whirl around, Asher pausing the game as he does so. His strawberry blond hair sticks out in every direction, matching Amelia's unkempt do. For someone so insistent on looking like a princess, she sure does have a thing against hairbrushes.

"That's not fair!" Amelia whines loudly. "Asher always wins because he's bigger."

"I win because I'm better," Asher corrects her, matching her shrill tone. "*And* bigger!"

"No, it's okay," I pipe up, using my quietest voice in hopes that it will encourage them to lower their own. "I don't want to play."

"No, Wylie, you get to go next," Dad insists, and I bend my neck forward until my nose is practically on my phone's screen, trying to make myself disappear. I hate when he does this—forces them to include me. Or really, forces me to include myself. To me, these visits had become nothing more than an obligation—a custody arrangement decided a dozen years ago by a judge who I would never know and who would never ask for my opinion on the matter. If asked, I would have put the kibosh on this plan—the one that makes me leave my actual town, actual home, actual parent, and actual life.

It takes me a beat to realize Dad is speaking to me. "What's that?" I ask him, glancing up from my phone.

"Would you rather do something else? We could go to the movies or miniature golfing? Or maybe—"

"No thanks," I stop him. "You don't have to entertain me." A crease appears across Dad's forehead, and for a second, I feel bad. "Thanks, though," I add quickly, even though what I want to say is I wish he would stop acting like I'm an out-of-towner to whom he is desperate to play tour guide. Rather than, you know, *his daughter*.

"We're planning on ordering Vietnamese food for dinner," Dad says. "Amy discovered a new place recently. Is that okay with you?"

"Sure," I answer. Ever since I mentioned that Mom is quite the experimental chef, Dad seems determined to compete, ordering a brand-new cuisine whenever I'm around, no matter Asher's and Amelia's protests. It's as if once Dad learned that I enjoyed tasting new foods, he had attached himself to this news like a barnacle. And while I know he means well, the more he tries to relate to me, the more I push him away. Even when I don't mean to, I can't seem to help myself.

"So you haven't?" I realize Dad is still talking.

"What's that?" I ask again.

"Have you tried pho?"

"Fah?" I repeat what he said. "Um, I don't think so. I don't know what that is."

"It's like a Vietnamese ramen soup," Dad says. "It's spelled *P-H-O*, even though it's pronounced 'fah.' That's what we're planning on ordering tonight."

"Sounds good." I force a smile. And while I'm mildly interested in trying pho, I also wish Dad would pull some boxed macaroni and cheese out of the pantry and slop it onto a paper plate with a hot dog and some wilted broccoli. That he would choose something that the four of them eat the rest of the week, on the days I'm not here.

Something that would make me feel a little less like a stranger at their kitchen table.

That evening, I take my seat between Asher and Amelia, a giant bowl of steaming soup waiting on each of our place mats. I examine it curiously: long spaghetti-type noodles wind their way through the broth, with thin pieces of chicken and vegetables sprinkled on top. I pull out my phone and snap a picture of the concoction before sending it to Jada, captioning it Pho, or today's attempt to bond with the extra daughter.

"Wylie, no phones at the table," Dad says as he sits next to Asher.

"I was sending Jada a picture," I say defensively, shoving the phone in my pocket.

"Looks good, doesn't it?" Amy asks. Her seat is next to Amelia and across from Dad. I sit at the head of the table, making clear that on nights I'm not here, the four of them sit in a perfect square. Boys on one side, girls on the other, the ideal family.

And then there's me, stuck onto the end like a mismatched extension cord.

"Why do we always have to eat weird stuff?" Asher asks, crossing his arms and slouching while poking the tip of his tongue through his missing front teeth. "I want pizza."

"I want pizza too," Amelia whines, which is her main mode of speaking.

"Soup is stupid!" Asher yells, his voice deafening.

"If you don't try it, you'll never know if you like it," Amy tells them calmly, in a much nicer tone than Mom would have greeted this kind of complaining. "See, Wylie is eating it."

Asher and Amelia both turn to me expectantly as I swoop the first spoonful into my mouth. And though

I don't appreciate being watched like this, I smile and nod obediently, proclaiming the pho "delicious" before opening my mouth wide for another taste, allowing the broth to drip down my chin.

At the sight of this, Asher and Amelia both dunk their own spoons into the pho, and without any more whining, they begin to eat. Dad and Amy watch them with pleased smiles, and I think I deserve a thank-you for convincing them that it's edible.

"We're going to have to start thinking about our Christmas card picture for this year," Amy says between slurps.

"It's barely October," I point out.

"Yes, but we should schedule time with the photographer for the next time you're here or the weekend after that," Amy says. "We probably should have booked him already—we don't have many Saturdays together before the holiday rush begins."

"I don't have to be in the card," I announce. "Seriously, I don't mind."

"Of course you're in the card," Amy says matter-of-factly. "We would never send the card without you."

"You can just put my name on it, then," I say. "I don't need to be in the picture. I promise it's okay."

I see Dad and Amy glance at each other, and I wonder if this has been discussed before. After all, I don't fit their theme. All of their names—Andrew, Amy, Asher, and Amelia—begin with *A*, and every year, they shift my placement in the signature. Sometimes I'm listed before Asher as the oldest kid, sometimes at the end as the "leftover." But no matter where my name falls, it sticks out from the rest. Compared to names like "Asher" and "Amelia," "Wylie" looks like it belongs to the family dog.

Though if they had a dog, no doubt it would be named Atticus or Abraham or something appropriately *A*-like. And he would most likely have strawberry blond fur, slightly gappy teeth, and his own permanent bed, which doesn't get hidden away whenever he's not around.

"You're in the card, Wylie," Dad says definitively. "It wouldn't be complete without our whole family." And while I understand that this is what he believes, it doesn't convince me that it's true.

★ 4 ★

That night, I sprawl out—or rather, I sprawl out as much as anyone can sprawl in a trundle bed—below Amelia's sleeping form. I lie on my stomach, my phone hidden beneath my pillow so the light doesn't wake her, and I open my text chain with Jada.

Hello??? I type. I'm dying here. Where are you?

After a few seconds, I see the dots that indicate she's writing back. Finally.

Sorry, she answers. What's up?

Did you see my Vietnamese dinner?

Oh, yeah, **she replies.** I assume you hated it.

The soup was good. But pizza also would have been good. Why does dinner always have to be such a production when I'm here?

Your dad's just trying to make you happy, right? **she writes, and I wince at her defense.**

I know that, **I begin,** but it makes me sooooo uncomfortable. It's like the more they try to make me feel included, the more I feel excluded. Like they're constantly calling attention to how I'm not here all the time by trying to be "welcoming." Plus, with the nonstop noise, it's like coming to a bimonthly torture chamber.

No offense, Wy, **Jada starts,** but don't you think that's a little dramatic?

I smirk. YOU'RE calling ME dramatic?

Shut it, **Jada says.** And speaking of dramatic . . .

Mason?

No, thank goodness. Actually, this might be better over the phone. Can you talk?

I'm lying next to a four-year-old, so no, **I say.** What's going on?

The reply dots pop on and off my screen over and over, and I can't imagine what Jada is typing. Spit it out already, **I tell her.**

I have an idea, **she responds eventually.**

Oh?

Remember what I was saying at lunch yesterday? About getting more involved in middle school life?

Yes? The back of my neck grows warm, and I drum my fingers against the back of the phone, oddly nervous. What exactly does Jada have in mind?

I want to audition for the musical, she writes. And I think you should too.

Absolutely not, I reply without giving it a second thought.

Oh, come on! You love to sing!

Correction: loved, I tell her. I told you, I'm not getting back on a stage. Not unless 100% necessary. Like graduation. Even picturing ascending a stage makes my lips pinch against my teeth, a pang of unpleasantness forming in my throat.

Wylie. That was THREE years ago. You need to get over it.

Says who? I ask, and I can almost hear Jada sighing through the phone.

You're being impossible, she says. But even if you won't, I'd like to audition.

Be my guest, I say, attempting to sound casual. When are they?

Tuesday after school.

Do you want me to come over tomorrow? I can help you prepare and pick songs or whatever, **I volunteer.**

We're going to my cousins' house, **Jada responds.** So I guess I'll see you Monday?

Otherwise known as COLBY'S PREMIERE DAY!!! **I remind her.**

How could I forget? And listen, if you change your mind about the auditions . . .

I won't, **I insist.** Good night. **I drop my phone onto the thin mattress as my wrists grow limp, deflated like a pinpricked balloon. Jada and I have gone through so much of our school lives as a pair that it's strange to imagine her doing something without me. Strange and a little bit scary. Because if Jada is about to become one of the theatre people, to join her own table in the cafeteria, then where will that leave me?**

I exhale as I flip onto my back and stare at the glow-in-the-dark stars on Amelia's ceiling, wishing for the cozy comfort of my own bed. Because few things are lonelier than lying awake in a room that is not your own, in a house that could not feel farther from home.

* * *

When I reach our lockers Monday morning, Jada is nowhere to be found. I lean against them, watching the bustle of the hallway pass while pulling out my phone to text her.

Where are you?

I wait a minute, then two, with no response. This isn't like Jada. She usually arrives before me. And if she's running late, she tells me, but I haven't heard a peep from her.

I wander down the seventh-grade wing, waving at Mrs. Nieska as I pass her door. I turn toward the front of the school, where I spot Jada's long licorice locks ahead of me.

Standing with the theatre people. At least eight of them. Maybe twelve.

I walk past their circle quickly and make a left, where I see Libby coming my way. And at this moment, I'm grateful to have someone—anyone—to talk to. As if to prove to myself that if Jada now has other friends, then I do too.

"Hi, Wylie!" Libby calls brightly, brushing the strands of her French braid back and forth over her fingers like a tiny broom. "Have a good weekend?"

"I did," I lie. "How about you? Did your grand-mother like her mailbox?"

"She loved it. Then I was supposed to spend the rest of the time preparing for the fall musical auditions, but I kept getting distracted."

"You're auditioning for the musical?" I ask, trying to shield the surprise in my voice. Is *everyone* auditioning for the musical?

"Shocking, I know," Libby says, wrinkling the freckles on her nose. "My dad thinks it would be good for me to join a group to 'find my niche' in middle school." She forms her fingers into quotation marks as she says this. "I figure I'll get cut immediately, but maybe they'll need someone to help with sets. I think I could handle painting a backdrop."

"Jada is auditioning too," I reveal.

"Does that mean you're auditioning?"

"No way." I shake my head adamantly.

"But what if she gets a part?"

"What do you mean?" I ask, even though in truth, I know exactly what Libby means. That Jada and I usu-ally do everything together. And if she's in the musical, then what will I do?

"You should audition," Libby declares instead of

answering my question. "That way, you'll be there for moral support when I look like a deer caught in headlights up there."

I shake my head again. "I'm definitely not auditioning."

"Why not? It could be fun."

"Trust me, it wouldn't be," I tell her. "Not for me. I'm someone who's meant to be in the audience, not onstage."

"I don't believe that," Libby says. "I remember when you and Jada sang Marquis Machine songs at school talent shows. You two were great."

At the mention of the talent shows, my toes curl in my shoes, as if they're trying to grip the floor more tightly. "I haven't sung in front of people since then," I say, not explaining the details as to why and hoping Libby doesn't recall.

"Then it's time to rip off the bandage! Come to my house later and we can prepare together. Or we can turn on the premiere of *Non-Instrumental* and *say* we prepared."

"Wait, you're watching that too?" I ask. "You know, I'm obsessed with Colby Cash."

"Oh, I remember," Libby says, but the morning bell

rings before she can elaborate. We take off in opposite directions, calling a fast good-bye, and my thoughts swirl like merging schools of fish. Maybe I should do it—audition for the musical. The stage incident, well, it *was* three years ago. Maybe I should get over it, move on, put it behind me. And then, if Jada and I are both cast, we could be in the show together. I could be friends with the theatre people too. We could all sit at the same table in the cafeteria, like the groups I've always admired. It could be ideal.

That is, of course, if I manage to stay on the stage.

★ 5 ★

I decide not to mention my thoughts about auditioning
to Jada, because if I do, she'll pressure me to follow
through, and I'm not yet ready to commit. Plus, it's
not like I have much opportunity to bring it up, since
Jada's face is perpetually buried in a large black binder
of musical materials.

"Remember. Seven forty-five. Not a minute later," I
remind her as we shuffle into the hallway after homeroom. "I have chips and salsa and those disgusting sour
gummy worms you like."

"Wait, what?" Jada asks absentmindedly. She stares forward, her eyes narrowed like she's concentrating on something miles away.

"Colby's big debut! Our scrapbook is already on the coffee table in preparation."

Jada comes to a sudden stop, hooking her thumbs through the loops of her jeans as if bracing for impact. "Don't be mad. . . ."

A prickly feeling fills my insides, migrating from my stomach to the tips of my fingers. "You can't back out," I tell her definitively.

"I'm not backing out. I'll watch it with you. I promise. But . . . I can't tonight. I need to practice for tomorrow, and I'm already behind." The flow of people pushes us forward, propelling us down the hallway like a riptide. The more seconds that pass without me responding, the more Jada seems desperate to fill the air.

"It's just that I want to memorize the script as much as possible," she rambles. "They didn't say it needs to be memorized, but I figure if I'm off book—doesn't that sound theatrical, 'off book'?—I'll have a better chance of getting a part. Most of these other people, they were in last year's shows. They have a leg up on me, so I want to make sure I'm as prepared as possible or else I may be—"

"We can't watch it later," I cut her off. "Colby's posting live throughout the show. It won't make any sense if we watch later."

"Watch it without me, then," Jada offers. "And then you can have a repeat viewing. You know you're going to want to watch him more than once anyway." I cross my arms against my chest, considering this. Jada had always been the one to freak out if I dared watch Marquis Machine's latest video or listen to their newest single without her. She had insisted that we experience their new material at the same time, hunched over a computer, eager with shared anticipation. Collectively, we had cooed over Colby and embraced every shred of information about him. This had been the norm for so long that I never pictured viewing his *Non-Instrumental* premiere alone.

"Come on," I plead. "Can't you take a one-hour break?"

"I really can't." Jada turns to me with a serious expression. "I want this, Wy. You understand that, right?"

"I do," I answer automatically, as if by reflex. "I just never thought you'd abandon Colby and me for the theatre people." I try to say this lightly, but I can't hide the edge in my voice.

"Oh, please. It's only one night. Don't act like I'm pulling a Mister Kitters on you." She nudges my elbow. "May he rest in eternal peace."

"Not funny," I tell her as we enter first period, but the corners of my mouth curl into a smile. Mister Kitters was my favorite stuffed animal—an orange-and-white cat with floppy paws and long whiskers. I credit Mister Kitters for making Jada and me friends, since on the first day of kindergarten, Jada walked over to meet him. For the first few weeks of the year, the three of us—me, Jada, and Mister Kitters—played together. But as the months wore on, he was included less and less. And eventually, the unthinkable occurred: Mister Kitters went missing.

To this day, I don't know what happened to him. I can't say if he was lost at home or school or someplace in between. And as sad as I was at the time (and honestly, part of me is still sad about it), I wasn't nearly as upset as I would have been if I hadn't made a new, real-life best friend, one who would never forget the shabby stuffed cat who had brought us together.

And that's the thing about Jada and me. We know all of each other's references because we've lived through everything side by side: new schools and new sib-lings; bad haircuts and bad grades; missing teeth and missing cats. Nothing is a mystery or requires a back-story, because we've been there for each other, present for every major life milestone, from nearly the very beginning.

So maybe the musical is it: the next big thing for us to experience together. After all, Jada was there, right beside me, the last time I'd walked onto a stage. Maybe with her next to me, I could find the courage to step onto onc again.

Libby is perched on my front steps, waving frantically, when I arrive home after school, and I'm surprised to see her waiting for me.

"Did you decide to do it?" she yells across the yard before I've pulled out my keys.

"The musical?"

"Of course the musical!" She scrapes her feet against the pavement as if performing a tap dance.

"You've been practicing, I see," I tease her, finish-ing the text I had been writing to Jada: If you change your mind and need a distraction, you know where I'll be at 8:00! "Do you want to come inside?"

"Do you have snacks?" Libby asks, and I look at her quizzically while unlatching the lock. "Sorry. My dad only keeps fruit in the house. 'If you're truly hungry, you'll reach for a banana.' Um, no, I will not."

"That is a tragedy," I tell her. "We have corn chips and salsa. And sour gummy—"

"You had me at 'chips,'" Libby says, breezing into the house behind me like she owns the place. She plops her bag on the kitchen table before depositing herself on one of the chairs, making herself at home, and I toss her the bag of tortilla chips.

"Yessssss," she says, dragging out the S for at least five seconds. Then through loud crunches, she adds, "I should come here more often."

I laugh, amused by the level of contentment on her face, and then I settle onto another chair. "You might not have time after you're cast as the lead in the musical."

"Talk about counting chickens before they're hatched," she says. "I don't think you're comprehending my level of singing ability. Or lack thereof."

"I'm sure it's not that bad."

"All I'm saying is that if I could sing like *you*, I certainly wouldn't be hemming and hawing about auditioning." She holds out the bag. "Would you like one of your own chips?"

I grab a handful and place them on the table in front of me. "It's not the singing that's the problem," I explain. "It's the stage."

"What about it?"

I take a deep breath. "If I tell you, do you promise not to bring it up again?"

"Cross my heart," Libby says, drawing an imaginary X over her chest.

"I'm not sure you remember the talent show in fourth grade. . . ." I begin. "Well, you would have been in third grade at the time, but Jada and I were performing a Marquis Machine song as a duet—"

"And you fell off the stage," Libby fills in.

"Um, uh, right," I stammer at Libby's casual tone. This is the number one most humiliating moment of my life, and she's acting like it's no big deal.

Libby waves her hand in front of her face dismissively. "Happens all the time," she says. "I'm sure no one even remembers."

"*You* remembered."

"I'm the exception to the rule," Libby says. "I'm sure no one but me, and Jada, and, well, *you* remember."

"And the music teacher. Who I landed on. She broke my fall."

"Still," Libby says. "Water under the bridge. If that's the reason you're afraid of auditioning, I think you should forget about it, because everyone else has."

"But *I* haven't forgotten. I haven't been on a stage since then, at least not to perform."

"Then that's the solution. The only reason the fall is so clear in your memory is because you haven't had a positive experience onstage since then. This audition could do the trick."

"Or it could make things worse," I say.

"*Or* it could make things better. Always look on the bright side!"

I sigh. "I'm thinking about it. I promise. But if you want me to help you prepare in the meantime, I'm happy to."

"Yes, please." Libby rummages in her bag, emerging with a beat-up-looking packet of papers. "Here. I guess we'd better read these."

"That's the script?" I ask. "Have you looked at it?"

"Not yet," Libby says with a sheepish grin. "Plenty of time." She flips through the papers. "Oh, whoops. I think I lost the last few pages somewhere along the way."

I giggle under my breath. "I have to tell you, all these years, I thought you had it together. You always seemed so organized, with your neatly braided hair . . ."

"It's all a farce," Libby says. "My hair is the only thing holding my life together."

"We may be in trouble, then," I tell her. "Since you know more about this audition than I do, and—no offense—you don't seem to know much."

"We may have bitten off more than we can chew. We're up a creek without a paddle."

I smirk. "Where do you come up with these expressions?" Libby covers her mouth, as if embarrassed.

"This is what too many afternoons at a grandmother's house will do. You start talking in old-fashioned clichés."

"You're a chip off the old block," I reply.

"Hey, look at you!" Libby says proudly. "I didn't think you'd be the type to have one on the tip of your tongue."

"You know what they say," I begin, "about not judging a book by its cover." Libby laughs uproariously at this, causing the freckles on her nose to crinkle like a wrinkly Dalmatian.

"Let's skip the boring paperwork and go straight to the fun part—songs," Libby says. "I think we can sing whatever we want. But we either have to do it a cappella, without accompaniment, or bring our own sheet music. And I don't suppose you have sheet music?"

"No, but what's wrong with a cappella?"

"Absolutely, positively nothing is wrong with a cappella," Libby answers emphatically. "Speaking of which, thank goodness *Non-Instrumental* returns tonight. I was starting to go through withdrawal."

"I've never watched it, but I'm excited to see Colby."

"Wait, you've never seen *Non-Instrumental*? Not one episode?" I shake my head. "No, no, no. This will never do. Fetch me a computer, please. Time waits for no man!"

"Is that another one of your grandmother's expressions?" I ask, grabbing the laptop from the counter and sliding it in front of her.

"Indeed. She has a million of them." Libby begins typing manically. "Let's start with my favorite group— Metronome Mayhem. Or wait, maybe you should see the original winners first. The Octavgenarians."

"What is with these group names?"

"Music puns," Libby says, placing the screen between us so we can view at the same time. I watch a group of four elderly men stroll to the center of the stage.

"How old are they?!"

"In their eighties," Libby answers. "They won the first season, and they also happen to be my grandmother's favorites. Though she thought they were a little 'long in the tooth.' Exact quote."

I laugh. "Let me see your favorites." Libby pulls up a Metronome Mayhem performance, and we both crane our faces toward the screen, me watching intently and Libby bouncing around to the beat. "You know, I never understood how this show has run for so many seasons. An a cappella group competition doesn't exactly sound like riveting TV, but this is kind of fantastic."

"Oh, it's not 'kind of' fantastic," Libby says. "It *is* fantastic."

"Has anyone ever performed a Marquis Machine song?" I ask.

"You have a one-track mind," Libby says with a smirk. "But yes. I'll find them. Maybe they'll give you inspiration for your audition."

"Maybe," I say innocently, and Libby widens her eyes.

"You're going to do it. I know you are," she says.

"And don't worry, if you fall off the stage, I'll roll down after you so that it looks like an avalanche."

"That's comforting," I tell her. And though I mean it sarcastically, I can't deny the fact that in some ways, it actually is.

★ 6 ★

Libby and I are still huddled over the laptop when Mom arrives home. "Hi, Wylie. Hi, Ja—oh hey, Libby!" she corrects herself, shooting me a questioning glance.

"Hi, Mrs. Tennyson!" Libby says brightly.

"So nice to see you," Mom tells her. "How have you and your dad been? We don't see you around the neighborhood much."

"We're good, thanks," Libby says. "And if Wylie and I both make the musical, you might be seeing more of me!"

"The musical?" Mom asks, eyebrows raised in surprise. "What musical?"

I open my mouth to speak, but Libby beats me to it.

"We're going to the fall musical auditions tomorrow," Libby explains, a mischievous look spreading across her face.

"That's not exactly—" I begin, but Mom claps her hands together, cutting me off.

"That's so great!" she exclaims.

"I don't—" I start, but Mom interrupts me again.

"I'm proud of you, Wy. I've been waiting for you to start singing again. Good for you for putting yourself out there!" I narrow my eyes at Libby, but my dirty look doesn't shake the gloating expression on her face as her phone begins ringing a calypso tune.

"One second; it's my dad," she says. "Hello?"

I stand up from the table, shoving three tortilla chips in my mouth as I approach the counter. This way, when Mom whispers, "The musical, eh?" I can point to my full mouth and not answer. Instead, I retrieve my phone to see if Jada has come to her senses and agreed that viewing Colby's show is more important than memorizing a silly script. But when I turn on the screen, rather than a barrage of messages, I find no texts, no calls, no questions. Nothing but a whole lot of silence.

The moment Libby returns home for dinner, Mom is on me. "Ready to explain?" she asks as she ladles soup into bowls. I grab silverware and napkins, salt and pepper, and milk, purposely skirting around her so as to not make eye contact.

"About what?" I ask sweetly.

"Wylie," Mom begins.

"Yes?" I sit with a *thump* and immediately raise a spoonful of soup. "Ouch!" I yelp as it burns my top lip, too hot for me to pretend that my mouth is full again.

Mom settles across from me. "You're auditioning for the musical?"

"Maybe. I haven't decided yet."

"I think you should." Mom stirs her own soup, the thick steam giving her face a blurry texture. "You've always liked to sing."

"I'm thinking about it."

"And it's good for you to get involved in activities."

"I said, I'm thinking about it," I repeat, breaking off

a hunk of bread and dipping it into the broth, hoping to keep my teeth occupied until the soup cools.

Mom puts her spoon down, focusing her attention on me. "Is something wrong?"

"Nope."

"Wylie."

"It's not!" I insist. "Nothing is wrong. Can we talk about something else?"

Mom retrieves her spoon. "Is Jada coming over tonight? Isn't it the big premiere?"

I shake my head. "She can't."

"Really? I thought you two have been waiting for this for weeks."

"She's getting ready for her audition," I tell her.

Mom puckers her brow. "For the musical?"

"Mm-hmmm." A trickle of soup sloshes over my bowl, and I use my pinkie to catch it.

"Jada's trying out too?" Mom asks.

"Yep."

"Is that why you're trying out?"

"I haven't decided if—"

"Why you're *thinking* of trying out?" Mom corrects herself.

I nod, and Mom looks down into her bowl as if

studying a magic eight ball. "Well, I think it would be great for you to try something new," she begins, "but I'm sure there are lots of activities for you to get involved in, with or without Jada."

"What's wrong with Jada?"

"Nothing's wrong with Jada. I love Jada. You know that. But I also know how she is, how she can sometimes, you know, take over a bit. I just don't think it would be a bad thing for you to broaden your horizons. You don't always have to get sucked into what Jada wants to do."

"So you don't want me to audition for the musical?"

"If *you* want to, then I think it's a fabulous idea," Mom says. "I'm only trying to make sure that you'd do it for the right reasons. And not because Jada told you to."

"She didn't tell me to," I say testily.

"Okay, then," Mom says. "For the record, I don't think auditioning could ever be a bad thing. It would be a good experience, no matter the outcome." She lifts a gigantic spoonful to her mouth and blows on it gingerly. "And believe me, I hope you and Jada are friends for the rest of your lives. It's just that you two often act like each other's safety nets—like you cling to one another so tightly that you're afraid of making a move without the other. And sometimes, it's good for friends to stand on their own."

I nod, pretending like I agree, but my mind is a flurry with one thought: that standing on her own, without me, is exactly what Jada is doing. She's auditioning whether or not I do. She's moving forward whether or not I follow her. And as my blank phone screen reminds me, it's hard to cling to someone who is already acting like she's forgotten you.

★ 7 ★

That night, I sit cross-legged on the couch, my phone balanced on my knee and Jada's unopened package of gummy worms sitting on the coffee table beside the scrapbook. My toes twitch anxiously, waiting for Colby's appearance, and I straighten my shoulders the moment he fills my screen. He's decked out in a blue velvet tuxedo with his hair combed into a high pompadour, and he would look mildly ridiculous if he weren't so exceptionally cute.

I lean forward to concentrate, grinning as he opens

his mouth to speak. But instead of an introductory monologue, Colby launches into song. No instruments, no music, no accompaniment—only his voice soaring across the studio. And no matter Jada's doubts about his potential as a solo artist, he sounds unbelievable.

Are you watching????? My phone vibrates with a text from Libby.

Yes! He's amazing!

I have to admit, I agree, Libby responds. This is the best season opener yet.

I'm so proud, I answer with a smiley face. As Colby throws to the first commercial break, I click out of the text chain and dial Jada, and she answers on the third ring.

"Mason is playing a kazoo out his bedroom window," she says without a hello.

"Colby is wonderful," I tell her, ignoring her complaint. "Are you sure you don't want to run over and watch the rest?"

"I can't. I'm not even halfway finished with the script, because it's a little hard to concentrate when someone is playing a *kazoo* across the lawn! Where could he have found a kazoo?"

I roll my eyes. "There's no kazoo playing outside of *my* house."

Jada grumbles unintelligibly. "So Colby is every-thing you dreamed he would be?"

"And more. I can't wait for you to see it. He sang the opening song a cappella."

"Cool," Jada says halfheartedly. "Anyway, speaking of a cappella, I really have to practice this. Talk tomorrow?"

"Wait." I stop her. "How about we make a deal?"

Jada sighs. "What kind of deal?"

"If you come watch *Non-Instrumental* with me right now," I begin, "I'll go with you to the auditions tomorrow."

"Hold on, you're going to try out too? What about your stage phobia?"

"If you watch Colby, I'll get over it," I say. "You're right—the talent show was years ago. I can't avoid the stage forever." And as I say this out loud, I'm not sure who I'm trying to convince more: Jada or myself. "So do we have a deal?"

"I can't, Wy. But you should come to the auditions anyway. They'll be fun."

"Ughhhhh," I groan as the commercials end and the camera zooms toward Colby. "I have to go; he's back on."

"Enjoy!" Jada hangs up, and while I try to refocus on the program, my mind keeps wandering back to the auditions. Because seeing Colby there, planted firmly in his spotlight and raising his voice for the world to hear, sends a firework of inspiration shooting through my veins. It reminds me of before: when I liked to sing, to perform, and to do so next to Jada.

I'll audition, I text her before I can talk myself out of it. Then I send the same message to Libby.

YAY YAY YAY! Libby writes back immediately. Broadway, here we come! (Or not).

Good girl, Jada answers a few minutes later.

We'll go together, right? I ask her. I need emotional support.

Sure, she answers, and instantly, I feel slightly better. Who knows? Maybe the auditions will go well. Maybe we'll both get parts in the show. Maybe it will be fun, for the first time, to be part of a larger group.

Together, just maybe, we can do anything.

But after school the next day, Jada is nowhere to be found. I wait by our lockers, but she doesn't appear, and my texts go unanswered. I hurry toward the auditorium and follow the other auditioners into the wings, where I stand on the tips of my toes, searching for her, but I don't spot her licorice locks anywhere. Especially because I can't seem to focus on much more than the three enormous beams of light shining onto center stage, bright and blinding.

And terrifying.

At once, all traces of confidence seep out of my body, spreading goose bumps up and down my arms. I cross them against my chest, trying to take deep breaths in order to calm the heavy beating of my heart. Where is she?

I turn around and weave through the crowd, pushing my way in the opposite direction, jamming into shoulders and knees and misplaced elbows. I need to retrieve my phone so I can text her again, so I can find out where she is, so I can stand next to her. There's no way I'll make it onto that stage if I don't.

"I've been looking for you everywhere!" Libby is suddenly in front of me, brimming with her typical enthusiasm.

And I have never been happier to see her.

"So are you ready for this? When I didn't spot you, I was afraid you bailed," Libby says.

"I almost did," I confess. "I can't find Jada, and I didn't expect so many people to be here, and the spotlights on the stage are so bright, and I still haven't decided what I'm sing—"

"Whoa." Libby holds up her hands, halting me.

"Okay, I get it—you're as nervous as a long-tailed cat in a room full of rocking chairs."

"As a what?"

"Yeah, that's one of my grandmother's best ones—I only whip it out on special occasions," Libby says. "Now buck up, champ. We can do this!" She links her arm through mine and pushes me toward the stage, leading me onto the choral risers until we come to a stop in the middle of the third row. I scan the crowd for Jada's face, but the spotlights overhead make me feel like a tractor trailer is barreling toward me, high-beams on full blast, and I can't see anything more than a foot in front of me.

Anything like the edge of the stage.

"I don't understand how they're going to get through everyone today," Libby prattles on. "Maybe we'll be delayed until tomorrow." I nod, though I can't imagine going through this again. I try to bend my knees, to settle into a comfortable position, but they feel locked into solid tree trunks, my toes beginning to tingle with pins and needles, followed by the tips of my fingers. I rotate my wrists in tense circles, but the movement, along with the lights above, starts to make me hot. I pull my hair off my neck, but then I'm chilled.

Is this what it feels like before you faint?

Where is Jada? Is she even here? I try looking around again, but my vision begins to blur. I close my eyes, but then the room starts to tilt to the right. I open them in a flash, finding that I'm clutching Libby's shoulder to steady myself.

"Are you okay?" she asks with a concerned look. I nod, but I don't release my grip.

"Welcome to auditions for the fall musical," the theatre director's voice booms across the stage, her heels clicking against the linoleum. "I'm pleased so many of you are interested in trying out, and I'm confident that with your help, we'll put on the best show possible!" And though I hear the words coming from her mouth and see her lips moving to match them, something feels disjointed. Like a television with a sound delay, her sentences swim into my mind from every direction, until I can't understand them at all.

"I've got to go," I whisper to Libby, stepping over her feet and then those of the girl next to her and so on and so on until I reach the end of the riser, where I jump onto the stage floor. Once I'm safely in the wings and out of the spotlights, my eyes sharpen, and I spot Jada staring at me from the first tier.

"What's going on?" Libby is suddenly next to me. "Are you okay?"

"Everyone who wishes to audition needs to be up here," the director calls after us. I glance at Jada, but she has turned away, her back toward me.

Without another thought, I run behind the stage and out the exit, where for the first time in many minutes, I'm able to catch my breath.

★ 8 ★

"What is the matter?" Libby has followed me out of the auditorium, crouching next to me as I lean against a wall, calming myself. "You went white as a marshmallow in there."

"Go back," I tell her. "You're going to blow your audition."

Libby waves her hand in front of her face, brushing off my instructions. "Not when you're out here looking like a ghost. Are you okay?"

I slide down to the floor. "I'm fine. Now go before the director doesn't let you return."

"No way," Libby insists. "I didn't want to audition anyway. I won't get a part over all those other people." She joins me on the ground. "So what happened in there?"

"I think it was the lights. I couldn't see the edge of the stage. I just—I don't know."

"It brought it back," Libby fills in. "It reminded you of the last time, and you freaked out. I get it. How about I go grab our bags, and then we get out of here?"

"Best idea you've ever had," I say. "Thank you."

Libby rises to her feet. "Now no disappearing acts while I'm gone," she says. "Actually, don't even try to stand. I'd rather you not have a head injury when I return."

I nod obediently as she vanishes through the door. And as grateful as I am for her assistance, I can't help but think about the person who didn't follow me off the stage, who didn't come check on me, who didn't seem remotely concerned.

Who didn't act one bit like the best friend she is supposed to be.

* * *

The next morning, after not receiving a single call or text from Jada, I've turned into a full-on mope. As last night wore on, the more time that went by without a word from her, the angrier I became. No, not even angry—hurt. She knew how anxious I was. She understood more than anyone my issues with getting back on the stage. And not only had she abandoned me, but when she saw that something was wrong, she didn't try to help. So I decide that if she isn't going to reach out to me, I'm not going to reach out to her either. I am stubborn in my resentment.

"Are you sure you're feeling okay?" Mom asks as our car crawls through the school drop-off line. "You don't seem yourself."

"I'm fine," I assure her. I haven't told Mom about the audition—if I do, she'll cart me off to a doctor and have me poked and prodded to figure out what's wrong with me when I'm already certain I know the issue: nothing but a lingering case of stage fright.

Well, stage fright and a missing best friend.

I kiss Mom good-bye as I exit the car, and then I walk into school and down to the seventh-grade wing. When I turn the corner to approach homeroom, I see

Jada at the end of the hall, standing in front of her locker and texting furiously.

Which confirms that her phone isn't broken. . . .

I straighten my posture as I approach, deciding what to do. Should I say hi first? Should I wait for her to speak to me? Why is it so complicated to be in a fight with your best friend?

Before I can decide, Jada glances up and catches my eye. I expect her to smile, to say something, to give me a nod of recognition.

Instead, she looks immediately back down to her phone.

What feels like a giant chunk of oatmeal sinks from my throat to my stomach, forming a knot of discomfort. I continue to my locker, ignoring Jada just as she dismissed me. We remain uncomfortably quiet as I begin swapping out my notebooks.

"The audition went great, thanks for asking," Jada eventually pipes up. I turn toward her slowly.

"Excuse me?"

"The audition went great," Jada repeats, slamming her locker door. "I appreciate your support."

Is she for real? Is she mad *at me*?

A hundred potential responses fly through my head. What can I say? How can I communicate how upset I am, how hurt I felt when she wasn't there for me and then didn't even check on me? How can I explain any of this when she doesn't think she's done anything wrong? When she has the guts to be mad *at me*?

Realizing my jaw is hanging open, as if anticipating my reply, I snap my mouth closed, turn around, and walk into homeroom, leaving Jada in the hallway alone.

Because if her current behavior calls for anything, it is a solid dose of silent treatment.

By lunchtime, Jada and I have not exchanged another word. I walk into the cafeteria tentatively and look toward our table, and despite myself, I'm relieved to see Jada in her usual place. I shuffle over and take my spot, keeping my eyes focused downward.

"I didn't know if you'd show up," Jada says.

"Where else would I go?"

"Well, you didn't seem like you'd want to eat with me."

"You didn't either. I thought you'd sit with the

theatre people." I rustle in my lunch bag, continuing not to make eye contact.

"If you keep not speaking to me, maybe I should," Jada retorts, taking an enormous bite of her sandwich as if putting a period at the end of her statement. But instead of giving in and apologizing or whatever it is she wants me to do (whether it's deserved or not, which it is *not*), I simply unwrap my own lunch, letting the sound of our chewing fill the space.

After a few silent swallows, Jada places her food down, crosses her hands in front of her, and faces me seriously. "I hate this. Can we stop?"

I look up and examine her face for a moment, trying to figure out if she's making a peace offering or continuing the fight.

"I'm not the one who started it," I reply, deciding to let her take it from there.

"You never asked how my audition was," Jada says. "After running out of it and making a big scene, you didn't think to check in with me."

"Check in with you?" I ask, incredulous.

"I told you how important it was to me. You could at least pretend to be interested." I stare at her, wide-eyed.

"We were supposed to go to the auditions together,"

I remind her, trying to stay calm. "You promised to stand next to me."

"I was nervous. I just wanted to get there and get started. You could've found me."

"*You* were nervous? How do you think I felt? The last time I was on a stage like that, I fell off of it!" I hear my voice rising.

"You didn't have to run away like that," Jada says coolly. "Just because I wasn't next to you."

"I almost fainted! That's why I ran!" I exclaim. "I thought I was going to pass out!"

Jada's expression softens ever so slightly. "I didn't know that," she says, more gently this time. "I thought you were throwing some sort of tantrum, getting back at me for not watching Colby's show or something. And then I never heard from you."

"And I thought you didn't care," I tell her honestly. "That you saw me flee the stage but never asked if I was okay."

Jada lets out a giant sigh. "So we're both jerks," she says. "And neither of us are jerks. Deal?" She holds out her hand. And though I don't exactly agree with how she has summed up the situation, I'm also ready to stop fighting. So I reach out my hand and shake hers.

"Deal. So how *was* the audition?"

"Argh, I've been dying to tell you," Jada says, her eyes dancing with delight. And though our handshake hasn't erased my hurt from earlier, I figure that sometimes you have to forgive in order to be forgiven, whether or not you need forgiveness in the first place.

★ 9 ★

In the middle of dinner that night, my phone begins dinging
with texts, one after another. I try to ignore them, abid-
ing by Mom's no-phones-at-the-table rule, but after the
fifth ding, my curiosity gets the best of me.

"What if it's an emergency?" I ask.

"Okay, fine," Mom relents. I sprint from my seat and
grab it, and I'm greeted by a string of texts from Jada.

I GOT A PART!!!!!! the first one reads. And then, The
one I wanted! I got Tallulah! I can't believe it! I'm so excited!
Arghhhhhhh!!!!

I look at the words, considering how to respond. I want to be happy for Jada—that's how a best friend should react. But being happy for her means being unhappy for me.

"Who is it?" Mom asks.

"Jada. I'll be right back."

Congratulations! I type. When can we celebrate?

Not sure.

Want to come watch the *Non-Instrumental* premiere? I offer. I saved your sour worms.

Can't, Jada writes back. Rehearsals start tomorrow. I have to prepare.

Okay. Well, congratulations again. I send her a smiley face before returning to the table.

"What was that about?" Mom asks.

"She had a homework problem," I lie, not ready to be on the receiving end of another barrage of questions about the musical. "I'm finished with mine, though, so okay if I watch TV?"

"Sure," Mom answers. "What are you going to watch?"

"*Non-Instrumental* again. Or at least Colby's parts."

Mom smiles. "If you would channel the energy you put toward being Colby Cash's biggest fan into something useful, you could truly be dangerous."

"Hey, Colby *is* useful," I insist, hightailing it for the living room. I collapse on the couch and scroll through our saved shows until I find Monday's episode.

I'm about to watch the premiere again, I text Libby.

So jealous, she replies. I already have a new favorite group.

Let me guess—the Staccato Skaters? The ones who only perform on roller skates?

ARE THEY NOT THE BEST? Libby responds, and I grin.

To be fair, COLBY is the best, I tell her. But they are pretty good. I tuck my phone under my thigh and press play, enjoying Colby's opening song for a second time and then a third. When the house phone rings, I turn up the TV's volume, but this only partially drowns out Mom's half of the conversation. And when I hear her say, "Well, if you're really in a pinch . . . ," I pause the recording to listen more intently. What is she agreeing to? "Yes, I'm off on Friday, so I'll be here when you arrive. And then Wylie will be home later."

Wylie will be home later for what?

I stand and hold my arms out on either side, palms raised, silently questioning Mom. But she has a blank expression on her face, which I know can only mean one thing: trouble.

Not me being in trouble, necessarily, but trouble in general. Something that Mom isn't happy about. And something that I almost certainly won't be happy about either.

I walk over and lean my ear against the phone receiver, trying to figure out who's on the other end, but Mom shoos me away. I roll my eyes and retrieve my own phone, where I find a new text from Libby: I wish Willow Oak had an a cappella group. I'm pretty sure I could handle just singing "dah" over and over. I hear Mom hang up, and I turn to face her.

"Well?" I ask. "What was that about?"

"Okay," she begins slowly. "Now don't freak out." Uh-oh. "We both have to be mature about this, because there's nothing we can do, and it'll be easier if we—"

"Just tell me," I interrupt her.

Mom grips the edges of the counter, steeling herself, her face tinged pink. "That was your father," she begins. "He was asking for a favor."

"Is he switching weekends? Because I don't want to go two weekends in a row, and—"

Mom shakes her head. "You're not going there. Your brother and sister—"

"They're my *half* brother and *half* sister," I correct her, but Mom ignores me.

"They're coming here."

I don't say anything at first, sure that I must be hearing things, positive that Mom is messing with me. Why would Asher and Amelia ever come here, to *my* house? They don't even know Mom. They barely know me. How is this appropriate?

"I know it's . . . not ideal," Mom continues. "Your dad knows that too. But they're in a bind. He and Amy have to go to a funeral overseas, and they can't bring the kids because they don't have passports. And any relatives who would normally watch them will also be at the funeral."

"So he asked *you*?" I ask dubiously.

"They're desperate," Mom explains. "I'm not thrilled about it either, Wy, but what could I say? *Leave them by themselves—I'm sure they'll be fine?*"

"Yes!" I shout. "Anything would have been better than saying they can come here!"

"It's only for a couple of days," Mom says. "Your dad will drop them off Friday afternoon and pick them up early on Sunday. Like I always tell you—we can handle anything for a couple of days."

"I don't want to handle it," I say, feeling unexpected tears welling up in the backs of my eyes, and I widen my gaze to prevent them from stumbling onto my cheeks. "Plus, I have plans this weekend. You didn't ask me first."

"You can still do what you need to when your brother and sister are—"

"They're not my brother and sister," I remind her.

"Wylie," Mom drones, a tug of impatience in her voice.

"I have plans," I insist. "I have things to do. I can't be playing host to those two terrors all weekend."

"What plans do you have?" Mom asks, and the way she's looking at me, I can tell she thinks I'm making them up.

Without missing a beat, I reply, "I'm starting an a cappella group." I state this with so much conviction that I almost believe it myself. "Libby and I are."

"Oh, you are, huh?" Mom asks, as if she knows this is a fib.

"Yes. And we have a lot to do to get it off the ground. We were planning on working this weekend."

"Well, like I said, just because Asher and Amelia will be here doesn't mean you have to cancel your plans. I'm sure they won't need entertainment twenty-four hours a day."

"Wait until you meet them," I grumble, turning to retreat to the living room.

"Wylie." Mom stops me. "I understand that this is not how you want to spend the next few days—trust me, if given the choice, I wouldn't want it this way either. But we have to make Asher and Amelia feel welcome. No matter how hard it is. Got it?"

I shrug my response. "I'll be as nice as I always am," I tell her cryptically, before turning my attention to my phone.

We should start one, I type to Libby. An a cappella group. Let's start one ourselves.

After I press send, I tap my fingers against the back of my phone, anticipating Libby's reply. She has to like the idea. She has to go along with it. She at least has to go along with it until the end of this weekend.

Moments later, my phone begins dinging with one text after another, all from Libby. One word at a time, with an exclamation mark after each, she has sent back:

BEST! IDEA! EVER! LET'S! DO! IT!

DAH DAH DAH DAH!

ALL! SING! ALONG!

★10★

Rather than Jada in front of my locker the next morning, I find Libby, bouncing up and down like a jack-in-the-box.

"The bathroom is around the corner if you have to go that badly," I tease her.

"You're never going to believe this," Libby says, ignoring my comment.

"Believe what?"

"I have the greatest news ever," she persists, still not revealing what said news is.

"Why didn't you text me if you were this excited about it?"

"Because I wanted to see your reaction in person," Libby answers. "So last night, I couldn't fall asleep because I was thinking about our a cappella group."

"Shhhh," I shush her. "Let's not spread that around yet." I push her gently to the side so I can reach my locker. "Now can you please tell me? I could use some good news right now."

"Fine, but I need full eye contact," Libby says. I keep my fingers on my locker dial but turn my face toward her, and Libby slaps her hands against her thighs in a mock drumroll.

"Yes?"

"Our group is going to be featured on *Non-Instrumental*!" she exclaims.

I stare at Libby blankly—has she lost her mind? How does she think our group—our group, which doesn't even exist yet—is going to be successful enough to compete in any singing competition, let alone a televised one?

"I know what you're thinking," Libby continues before I can respond. "I'm not talking about competing on the show."

"Thank goodness," I tell her. "I thought you had lost your marbles."

"Good cliché, by the way," Libby says. "Anyway, late last night, on the *Non-Instrumental* website, they posted an advertisement for a contest. The show is searching the country for new a cappella groups—ones that were inspired by watching *Non-Instrumental*."

"Libby," I say slowly. "We don't even *have* a group yet. We can't win a singing contest without actual singers."

"It's not part of the competition," Libby continues, unperturbed by my reasoning. "It's for a promo piece about the show's influence in the a cappella world."

"That's all well and good, but it doesn't matter if—"

"Wait, I didn't get to the best part," she stops me. "Besides a feature in the promo, the groups that are picked will also get a video call with . . ." She pauses as I turn back to my locker. "Hey, I need your full attention!"

I drop my hand and make a slow pivot to the left. "Go ahead," I say doubtfully.

Libby waits a few seconds for dramatic effect before thrusting her arms in the air and yelling, *"Colby Cash!"* All at once, I feel the skin on my face pull downward as my chin crashes toward the floor.

"You're making that up," I say. "I looked at his posts this morning, and there was nothing about this contest."

"I swear it's true!" Libby squeals. "It went up superlate—maybe he's not awake yet on California time? Anyway, is that not the best news ever? It's like the contest is meant for us!"

"It's pretty amazing," I tell her, not wanting to dampen her enthusiasm. "But realistically, how can we possibly . . ." I finally pry open my locker and am greeted by an onslaught of Colby's face.

"Whoa," Libby says, sticking her whole head inside to examine my work more closely. "You mean to tell me you're creating these kinds of Colby Cash tributes, and you're not *ecstatic* over the prospect of a phone call with him?"

"Of course I want the call. But how long would we have to pull this together?"

Libby scrunches her face to the side. "Two weeks."

"Two weeks?!" I exclaim. "Libby, that's impossible."

"No, listen. The deadline is two full weeks from today," she clarifies. "That's fourteen whole days. We can do it."

"Stop." I halt her. "There's no way."

"We need to try," Libby argues. "What's the worst that

can happen? We don't win? No, the worst that can happen is that we don't even *attempt* to win. You can't swim without getting in the water! We need to get in the water!"

I sigh, suddenly exhausted. "I'll think about it."

"No thinking about it," Libby insists. "Just *doing* about it."

"I don't even know where to start. I'm not kidding. I have *no idea* where to begin."

"Do you know anyone on Student Council?" Libby asks as the homeroom bell rings. "Sixth grade hasn't elected officers yet, but someone from yours should know how to start a new group." With that, she takes off down the hall, calling, "Text me updates!" over her shoulder. I slump into homeroom, feeling like a gorilla is balancing on my shoulders. I don't have the first clue about starting an a cappella group, and clearly, Libby doesn't either. Even with the promise of Colby dangling like a golden carrot in the distance, I can't imagine how we can pull this off. So maybe we shouldn't do it. Maybe it would be best to give up before we're faced with the inevitable disappointment.

But then my mind flashes forward to this weekend, to Asher and Amelia running around my house, infiltrating my space, touching my things, with nowhere for me to escape. Even if our plan is unattainable, Libby is right—we have to try.

At least, we have to try until this weekend is over.

As our homeroom teacher takes attendance, I pull out my phone and text Jada, Who do we know on Student Council? I look up and see her glance away from her giant black musical binder to her phone screen.

Um, besides Mason? she writes back.

He is?

Treasurer, I think, she responds. I certainly didn't vote for him.

I need to ask him a question, I tell her. Don't freak out about it.

Blech, just leave me out of it, she answers, and I see her place her phone in her pocket and return her attention to the gargantuan binder. I stroll over to Mason's desk, hoping he'll make this as painless as possible. He watches me curiously as I approach, his lips spreading into a nosy grin.

"Question for you," I launch in before he can speak. "You're the class Treasurer, right?"

"Vice President, but thanks for demoting me," Mason responds, the smile growing wider.

"Even better. Do you know anything about how school activities work? Like if someone wants to start a new group, do you know how to go about that?"

"Is this someone you?" Mason asks.

"Do you know what the process is?" I ignore his question. "Or someone who would know?"

"What kind of group are you starting?" he asks.

"I never said I was—"

"Come on—secrets are no fun." He props his chin in his hands with a mischievous look.

I cross my arms. "Fine. An a cappella group. My friend and I want to create one."

"Jada?"

"No, another friend."

"You have another friend?" Mason asks in a teasing tone.

"Can you help me or not?"

"I can," he says. "The first thing you need is a faculty advisor. All school-sanctioned groups require one. So if you choose a teacher to help lead the activity, he or she should be able to take it from there."

"Thank you," I tell him, beginning to walk away.

"Hey, wait a minute," Mason says. "Keep me posted, okay?"

"Why?"

"Why not?" Mason responds playfully. I roll my eyes high and return to my seat, shuffling through my mental Rolodex of teachers. Choosing one of the music teachers would make the most sense, but they already have a lot of activities to run. And if we want to get this a cappella group together quickly, we need someone who isn't in charge of any other after-school events. Someone who won't question why, yes, we need to start immediately, and no, this isn't only about getting me one-on-one time with Colby Cash.

Someone like Mrs. Nieska.

★11★

Not only does Mrs. Nieska agree to be our faculty advisor, but she looks ten times more enthusiastic about it than I've ever seen Mrs. Nieska look about, well, anything.

"I can't believe the school hasn't had its own a cappella group before," she says. "Some of my fondest memories are from my a cappella group in college."

"Wait, you were in an a cappella group?" I ask.

Mrs. Nieska stares at me over her glasses with arched eyebrows. "Yes. I assumed that's why you asked me."

"Well, now I know for sure that you're the perfect choice!"

She smiles. "I always thought Willow Oak should have one, but I wasn't sure if students would want to participate."

"Yeah, I'm still not positive they will. . . ." I tell her sheepishly.

"I have faith. I'll pick up the correct forms from the office so we can get ourselves on the books. Do you have plans for how to recruit?"

"My friend and I are going to work on it tonight and over the weekend. I guess posters and fliers? Is there anything else you can think of?"

"If I do, I'll let you know," she says. "Thanks for asking me, Wylie. I'm excited."

"Me too. Thank you for taking it on!" I text Libby the news as soon as I leave the room.

Awesome! she writes back. Four members to go until we're eligible for the show.

I read her text twice before responding, Huh?

Groups need to have at least six members to enter the contest.

You left out that detail, I send her.

Oh, please. We should be able to find four people in no time!

I look up, scanning the hallway as if searching for a potential new member. Unlike Libby, I fear recruiting four people will be incredibly hard, especially in such a short time frame.

But at least I have a project to work on this weekend, an excuse to get out of the house, a good reason not to pay attention to the unwelcome visitors. And therefore, no matter what happens in the long run, for the time being, Project Colby Cash Video Call is one hundred percent a go.

After a full day of listening to musical updates from Jada—about people I don't know, let alone care about—I'm grateful for Libby's chatty a cappella–related banter as we sort through her basement's treasure trove of craft supplies.

"This place is insane," I tell her. Glitters and glues and poster boards and markers and feathers and pompoms and countless other items take up an entire wall, stacked like a do-it-yourself paradise.

"I can't resist a craft store," she says.

"Where does the plate smashing happen?"

"My dad has relegated that to the back room," she says, pointing. "Would you like to give it a whirl?"

"Maybe later. We should probably get to work. Are you up for taking charge of the posters?"

"Sure," Libby says. "And you'll do the fliers?"

"Do you have a computer I can use?"

"Yes, there's a program on my laptop," Libby says. "Follow me." We carry piles of supplies upstairs and spread out in the family room, me perched on the recliner with the computer and Libby sprawled on the carpet surrounded by poster boards. I stare at the blinking cursor and Libby at the blank canvases, neither of us knowing where to begin.

"I guess we need a name?" I start.

"Yes, that would help. I brainstormed during the day but nothing stuck."

"I'll search for a list of musical words." I begin typing.

"I guess 'The Music Notes' is too simple, huh?" Libby asks. "And corny?"

I scrunch my nose and shake my head. "How about The Trebleizers? Then we could use the treble clef for our symbol."

"The Treble Tones won *Non-Instrumental* a few years ago. I think it's too close to that."

"Okay. The Minuet Meisters?"

"Are we singing Mozart?" Libby teases.

I smile. "Good point. Do we even need a name? Maybe we should be 'Willow Oak Middle School's A Cappella Group.'"

"Snooze. No way *Non-Instrumental* will pick a group with a name like that." I drum my fingers against the keyboard, thinking, while Libby taps out a rhythm with her markers.

"Wait, I've got it," I say. "'Off the Stage.' Get it? Because we're never going to perform on a stage."

"You haven't mentioned that little tidbit."

"Oh, come on. You saw what happened at the auditions. We can get by with performing only on nonraised surfaces."

"We'll cross that bridge when we come to it," Libby says. "Now keep thinking."

We brainstorm quietly for a few more minutes before I suggest, "Maybe we should wait until we have a group to pick a name. Other people might be more creative."

"No one is going to join a group without a name. It's bad marketing."

I look at her quizzically. "You know about marketing?"

"It's part of my dad's job. I pick up a little here and

there. Anyway, why are we making it so complicated? Let's pick a word that's related to music and pluralize it." She stands and begins pacing the room. "The Arias? The Symphonies? The Operas?"

"They sound very serious," I say. "We want to give the impression that we're fun—that joining would be a break from regular life, instead of being another obligation." I sit back, peering at the ceiling to think. What's a term in music that symbolizes all of that in one word? "The Rests" doesn't have much ring to it.

"The Finales?" Libby offers. "Like 'Save the best for last; here come The Finales!'"

"That's not bad," I say, typing. "It looks a little funny written out, though. It may be too close to 'finals'—and no one wants to be reminded of finals."

"Definitely not."

"Hold on," I say, suddenly excited. "I think I have it." I raise a fist in the air triumphantly.

"Spill it!" Libby hops over three poster boards until she's in front of me.

"The Intermissions," I reveal grandly. "An intermission is a break in the middle of a show, and we're a break from regular life. What do you think?" Libby stands statue still, and for a moment, I fear the name is less brilliant than I thought. "Do you like it?" I prod her. "Or no? I mean, we can keep brainstorming—"

"I don't like it," Libby cuts me off. "I *love* it. It is beyond perfect!" She holds both hands out, and I high-ten her happily. "Now let's get to work!" Libby returns to the floor, grabs a silver marker, and scrawls THE INTERMISSIONS in giant bubble letters across the first poster. "Get ready, Colby Cash! Here come The Intermissions!"

★12★

Libby and I arrive at school extra-early Friday morning carrying six colorful posters and a bushel of fliers. At the bottom of each, we've written, "Make your own music, find your own voice!" with information about our first practice on Monday. Mrs. Nieska appears in the seventh-grade wing as we're positioning the final poster, and she peers at it over her glasses. Her face is stoic in a way that makes me nervous, as if Libby and I have done something wrong. But then she breaks into a huge grin, nodding with approval.

"You two did an amazing job with these," she says. "I spotted them all over school—they're so eye-catching!"

"That's Libby's doing." I point to her. "Have you met Libby, by the way? Libby, this is Mrs. Nieska. Mrs. Nieska, Libby."

"Nice to meet you!" Libby chirps. "Thank you so much for being our faculty advisor!"

"It's my pleasure," Mrs. Nieska says. "As I told Wylie, a cappella holds a special place in my heart. And the name you girls have come up with? Stupendous."

"*That* was all Wylie," Libby tells her. "I don't see how *Non-Instrumental* can turn us down with a name like that." I shoot her a look, silently shushing her. I hadn't told Mrs. Nieska about the contest yet. I was afraid that if she figured out that our main motivation is to win a call with Colby Cash, she wouldn't take us seriously. But unfortunately, Libby is paying no attention to the *be quiet* eye daggers I'm throwing her way.

"We have to be one of the youngest groups they've ever seen," she continues.

Mrs. Nieska smiles. "Yes, who knows? If you keep this up, maybe I'll see you on there in a few years."

"Or in a few weeks," Libby responds, and it's all I

can do not to place my hand directly over her mouth.

"You're very ambitious, aren't you, Libby?" Mrs. Nieska asks kindly. "I do hope that a lot of people show up on Monday."

"Or at least four," Libby replies, and I roll my eyes behind their backs, giving up.

"So on Monday," Mrs. Nieska continues, thankfully not seeming to notice anything odd about Libby's comment, "are we holding auditions? Or can anyone join?"

"We'll take whoever we can get!" Libby answers.

"I agree, no auditions," I say. "I think the process should be stress-free."

"Sounds good," Mrs. Nieska says, turning in the direction of her classroom. "I'll see you girls later— pleasure to meet you, Libby!"

"You too!" Libby calls.

As soon as Mrs. Nieska is out of earshot, I whisper-yell, "I haven't told her about the contest yet. So keep that on the down-low."

"Why?" Libby asks. "That's our big selling point for getting others to join!"

"I didn't want her to think we were only doing this because of Colby, or to get on TV, or whatever. We can tell her about the contest once we actually have a group."

"So we're not mentioning it to the people who show up on Monday either?"

"I don't think we should. I say we keep the plan between us for now." The first bell rings, opening school for the day.

"Okay," Libby says. "Here, give me a stack of fliers. I'll force them on some sixth graders." I hand her the top half of the pile.

"Good luck," I tell her.

"You too!"

I walk toward my locker, lifting the flap of my bag and trying to jam the fliers inside. SMACK. I bang into the figure in front of me, and the fliers fall from my arm and flutter down the hallway.

"I'm so sorr—Oh, it's you." I begin to apologize before I spot Mason before me, his baseball cap more askew than usual.

"Way to keep your eyes on the road," he says, a smirk unfastening his lips.

"I could say the same for you," I retort, stooping down to gather the fliers before they get trampled. And to my surprise, Mason bends down to help me.

"This is the group you were referring to yesterday?" he asks. "The Intermissions?"

"Yes."

"An a cappella group?"

"Yes," I say again. "No need to make fun of it."

"How many members do you have so far?" He hands me the fliers he's gathered, keeping one for himself.

"Why do you ask?" I'm instantly suspicious.

"Just curious," he says, scanning the paper as we reach our locker bank. "I think I know some people who would like to join."

"Oh, yeah? Who?"

"Remember, I have my finger on the pulse of this school," Mason says, his eyes dancing with amusement. I cross my arms and tilt my head.

"I'm sure you think you do."

"You don't believe me?" he asks.

I push my bangs out of my face, trying to decide what he's up to. "Why would you help? What's in it for you?"

"Well, I certainly can't join a group without any members. That would be embarrassing. I have a reputation to protect."

"Wait, you're joining?"

Mason shrugs. "Seems like fun." He strolls into homeroom without further comment.

And I don't know whether to be excited or horrified

that The Intermissions now have three members . . . and that one of those members is Mason Swenson.

Jada has been so preoccupied with the musical that I've barely had a chance to talk to her since she was cast—or, in actuality, I've barely had a chance to talk to her about anything other than the musical. When we get to lunch, she mercifully sets her ever-present script binder to the side—not out of sight, but at least no longer the main focus.

"What are you doing this weekend?" she asks in what seems like the first question she's posed to me in days.

"Asher and Amelia are coming," I tell her casually as she unpacks her food, and she doesn't react, proving she's not paying attention. "Did you hear me?"

"Asher and Amelia are coming," she repeats like a robot. "Wait, what? They're coming to *your* house?"

"Yes."

"But why?"

"Ugh," I groan. "It's a long story. One that begins and ends with ruining my weekend."

"Why are they coming? For how long? Where are they going to sleep?" she rattles off.

"Not with me, that's for sure. They're supposed to

bring sleeping bags and camp out in the living room. So I plan on barricading myself in my bedroom."

"How did your mom agree to this?"

I roll my eyes. "You know how she is. She felt bad. I would have never agreed, if anyone had asked me."

"That's outrageous," Jada says. "Sorry I won't be around to save you—we have rehearsal all weekend. When do they arrive?"

"They'll be there when I get home today. I'll have no reprieve." I start searching my bag for my water bottle.

"What are those?" Jada asks, pointing. I follow her finger to the neon papers peeking out between my books.

"Fliers about The Intermissions. We haven't had a chance to talk about it yet, but I'm—"

"Wait, the new a cappella group?" Jada asks, and I'm impressed she's already heard about it—our marketing must be working. "You're joining that?"

"Kind of. I mean, I started it. With Libby, so it would be weird if I weren't in it. . . ."

Jada's eyes grow wide. "You *started* the a cappella group? Why didn't you tell me?"

"It just happened," I explain. "Libby and I came up with the idea a couple days ago. And you and I haven't exactly had much time to chat."

"Who's in the group?" Jada asks immediately. "You and Libby and who else?"

"I don't know yet. Believe it or not, Mason mentioned that he would like to join, but it's hard to tell if he's being serious."

"Mason?!" Jada gags on his name. "You're starting an a cappella group with Mason?"

"I'm not starting it *with* him—I'm starting it with Libby," I say evenly. "I can't stop him from joining if he wants to."

"Of course you can!" Jada insists. I search her face, trying to figure out if she's kidding, but she looks scarily intent. "I'm your best friend," she continues. "You're supposed to be loyal to me. Not to my sworn enemy."

"Oh, please. I'm always loyal to you," I respond, growing increasingly frustrated.

"You're not, if you're going to start hanging out with the person I can't stand most in this world. You can't be friends with me and with Mason. You need to choose."

"Choose?" I can barely believe what I'm hearing. "You want me to choose who I socialize with? What if I said the same thing to you?"

"You can socialize with anyone you want. Except

Mason Swenson. If you were loyal to me, you would know that."

"Loyal to you? You're the one who hasn't been loyal!" I erupt, any trace of calmness vanished from my voice. "You joined the musical without me. You left me alone on the stage when you knew I was scared. You've barely spoken to me in days, and when you do, it's only about your show." My voice reaches such a crescendo that people start glancing in our direction. More quietly, I continue, "This is my a cappella group. As much as you may try to make it about you, like you love to do, it will never be true."

For a second, Jada looks like she's been stung, a flash of hurt shooting across her face. I expect her to start crying, or to start apologizing, or to start insisting that we end this fight immediately. But instead, she rises to her feet, grabs her belongings, and says one word: "Fine." With that, she marches across the cafeteria to the theatre people's table and takes a seat at the end of the bench.

And not once, not even for a moment, does she look back.

★13★

Jada and I manage to avoid each other for the rest of the
day, and the moment the final bell rings, I fly out the
front door while texting Libby.

Should I come over so we can brainstorm? I'm not really
in the mood to work on The Intermissions, but I'm even
less in the mood to deal with Asher and Amelia.

Can't today. Have to go to my grandmother's, Libby
writes back. Tomorrow?

Okay, I answer with a sigh, and I wonder how many
times I can circle the neighborhood before Mom sends

out a search party. As slowly as possible, I drag myself home, half-guilty for leaving Mom alone with them for longer than necessary and half-debating how I can further delay my arrival. What I feel like doing right now is curling up on the couch, a blanket over my knees and the scents of Mom's exotic Friday-night cooking wafting through the house. I don't want to think about Jada or The Intermissions or Mason. I don't want to think about anything. I want to be quiet, calm, and as far away from the terrors as possible.

I reach my house entirely too soon, bracing myself for noise, chaos, and pure annoyance. I take a deep breath before turning the key, and once the door is open a crack, I consider darting upstairs to my room and locking myself in. But as irritated as I am with Mom, I can't bring myself to abandon her completely. So I close the door softly behind me, and I listen. For a moment, it's so quiet that I wonder if—fingers crossed—Dad found someone else to watch them, and they're not here after all. Tentatively, I peer into the kitchen.

"Wy? Is that you?" Mom's voice greets me, and I'm forced to reveal myself.

"It is." I try to say this cheerfully but am not entirely

successful. I find Mom, Asher, and Amelia gathered around the table playing one of my old board games.

And it is quiet. Eerily, pleasantly quiet. No yelling, no whining, no screams of *no fair!* or *my turn!* or *he's cheating!* The scene is almost picturesque.

Then, without warning, Amelia leaps off her chair, runs across the kitchen, and throws her arms around my waist—tightly. Never before has Amelia looked so happy to see me—and never before, as far as I can remember, have we hugged.

"Hi, Amelia," I greet her, gripping her shoulders with surprise. "Hi, Asher."

"Hi, Wylie," he answers politely, and though he doesn't envelop me in a bear hug, he, too, looks more pleased than usual by my presence.

"How was your day?" Mom asks as Amelia relinquishes her hold.

"Okay," I answer. "How are things around here?"

"Great," Mom says. "We're thinking pizza for dinner—how does that sound?"

"Awesome," I answer, mildly amused that, for once, I'm getting the kind of Friday night I've always coveted: pizza, board games, and a bustling family.

Even if that family includes Asher and Amelia.

                              *   *   *

I'm shocked that throughout dinner, the terrors remain
on their best behavior. It seems that once they're out
of their element—away from their parents, their house,
and their comfort zone—they're much mellower. They're
even somewhat enjoyable.

"They were so relieved when you arrived," Mom
whispers as we clean up. "I'm proud of you for being a
good sister to them. It's clear they love you very much."

"They can sleep on the floor of my room, if that will
be better," I tell her quickly, before I can think better of
it. "Not in my bed—I have my limits—but if you think
they'll be more comfortable in there, that's okay."

"I'm sure that will make them much happier," Mom
says, giving my hand a squeeze. "If you finish in here,
I'll get them settled." She gathers their things and herds
them up the steps while I finish packaging the leftover
pizza. Then I search through my bag until I find my
phone, hoping, more than I would like to admit, to find
a text from Jada. But there's only one message waiting
for me, from a number I don't recognize.

Do you know Abigail and Audrey? I read. They're in 8th
grade—not sure of their last names. I spoke to them after school,
and they're interested in joining the group. They said they're

                                                          105

going to find you on Monday to ask some questions, but I think they're in.

I read the message again, trying to figure out who it could be from. Mrs. Nieska? I'm pretty sure teachers don't text students. Is Libby texting from her dad's phone? That seems unlikely. Who could this be?

Sorry, I respond, but who is this?

Mason.

Mason?!

Um, how did you get my number? I ask.

You put it on the flier, Mason reminds me. Boy, you don't trust me at all, do you?

I feel my face grow warm with embarrassment. Whoops, forgot about that, I reply. But great news about the 8th graders. I'll speak to them on Monday.

Just don't do anything weird and scare them off, Mason writes with a winking face. You know, like accuse them of gathering your personal information behind your back.

I'll do my best, I reply, smiling to myself. So you're really planning on joining?

Mason takes a second to respond and then writes, Is that okay?

Sure, I answer. But what's with the sudden interest in singing?

I could ask you the same thing, **Mason answers.**

Are you any good?

I guess you'll have to wait and see, huh? **he writes cryptically.** Have a good weekend.

Perplexed, I open Libby's text chain and send her an update. So Mason Swenson (of all people) found two 8th graders who want to join The Intermissions. They're supposed to talk to me on Monday, but he seems confident they're in.

Yay! **Libby writes back.** How about we do a Non-Instrumental marathon tomorrow? We could use the old seasons as inspiration.

Would love to, but may have to postpone until Sunday, **I answer.** Can I let you know?

Sure. Night, night.

Amelia appears in the kitchen then, decked out in a pair of princess pajamas. "Will you read me a book?" She looks up at me innocently.

"Sure. I'll show you where the bookshelf is so you can pick one." She grabs my hand, and I hear myself volunteering, "How about a piggyback ride?"

With a gappy grin, Amelia climbs aboard and grasps her arms firmly around my neck. And when we reach my room and I deposit her in a giggling heap on my bed, it appears that, for once, neither one of us feels like whining.

★14★

When I wake up the next morning, I'm startled by the sound of faint breathing before remembering that Asher and Amelia are here. I stretch out in bed and reach for my phone, where there's still no word from Jada. I hate not speaking to her, but I also don't think I'm entirely wrong. Maybe I said some things I shouldn't have, and I would be willing to apologize for them.

But only if she apologized first.

I slip off my bed and walk as quietly as possible toward the door. Amelia is missing from her sleeping bag, but Asher is tightly snuggled within his, only the tips of his strawberry blond hair peeking out the top. I'm about to step over him when something catches my eye: a small fur-like tuft. I peer down for a closer look, and before I can stop myself, I gasp—loudly.

This gasp causes Asher to sit up straight, the sleeping bag covering his form like a bloated caterpillar.

"How did you get that?" I shriek, suddenly not able to control the volume of my voice.

"What?" Asher asks groggily.

"This!" I shout, reaching down to snatch Mister Kitters. "How did you get *this*?"

"It's mine," Asher says, his eyes widening into a more alert stance. "Give him back!"

"He is *not* yours! And I want to know where you found him!"

"He's mine!" Asher insists as Mom flies through the door, Amelia at her heels.

"What's wrong?" Mom asks, examining the scene, and I hold out Mister Kitters. "Wow, Mister Kitters. I haven't seen him in ages."

"He's mine!" Asher yells, now matching my rage.

"He's *mine*!" I yell back, not caring how juvenile I sound. "You stole him!"

Asher shakes his head back and forth ferociously, shimmying out of his sleeping bag before jumping in the air to try to snatch the cat away.

"That's Fluffy," Amelia pipes up. "He's Asher's snuggly. Mine is Feather." She walks to her own sleeping bag, reaches deep inside, and emerges with a dingy-looking stuffed bird.

"His name is Mister Kitters, not Fluffy," I tell them. "Fluffy is a dumb name." But as I'm arguing this point, in a flash, Asher leaps onto my bed and grabs Mister Kitters out of my raised arm. "Hey!" I squawk, throwing myself on the mattress to tackle him, but he rolls off and hides behind Mom, Mister Kitters hugged securely to his chest.

"Mom," I say as calmly as possible. "Tell him."

Mom is rubbing her forehead, creating wrinkles that hadn't been there a few seconds ago. "It sounds like this is all a misunderstanding," she begins slowly. "Wylie, you must have left Mister Kitters at your dad's house when you were little, and they assumed he was Asher's."

"But he wasn't," I remind her.

"But in the meantime," Mom continues, ignoring me, "Asher has clearly grown attached to him. So I think it would be nice if you let this go and just be happy that Mister Kitters is being loved."

I can't believe what I'm hearing. Dad, I would expect to take Asher's side. Amy, obviously. But Mom? Mom is *my* mother. If there's anyone's side she should be taking, it's mine.

"For right now," Mom continues when I don't respond, "why don't you let me hold on to Mister Kitters—er, Fluffy—for safe-keeping." She looks at Asher, who examines her through narrowed eyes before eventually handing him over. "Thank you. Now, I'm making French toast, so how about we go have a good breakfast?"

Instead of answering, I step around Mom and out of my bedroom, stomping down the hall and then the stairs. I collapse on the couch, gripping my phone and ready to text Libby to please—*please*—save me immediately.

Which is when I notice the massacre on the floor in front of me.

Next to the coffee table, surrounded by dozens of crayons, lies Jada's and my Colby Cash scrapbook. Open, pages askew, with Amelia's preschool writing scrawled over the plastic coverings. Multicolored squiggles decorate the entries like hideous graffiti, and I am so flabbergasted by the sight that when I open my mouth to scream, no sound escapes.

I gather the scrapbook in my arms and step over the strewn crayons, breaking some in the process. I fly into the kitchen and nearly run into Mom, neither Asher nor Amelia in sight.

"Look!" I manage to sputter, my lips tight with anger. "Look what she did!"

I hold the ruined scrapbook up for her to examine, and Mom's eyes stretch with panic. "Oh . . . dear. I didn't know—"

"How could you let her do this?" I screech. "Why weren't you watching her?"

"I was making breakfast," Mom says. "I had given her some of your old coloring books, but I guess she spotted that on the coffee table. I'm so sorry, Wylie. It was an accident."

"It *wasn't* an accident! She should know better than to write on someone else's property."

"She's only four," Mom tells me, like I don't know her age.

"Why do you keep defending them? You should be defending me!"

"I'm not defending anyone. I understand you're upset. I do. But in a few years, I bet you and Jada will find this funny."

"It's *not* funny," I insist, my teeth chattering with fury. "It's not funny at all."

Mom sighs as if I'm the one being irrational. "I think you need to keep this in perspective. No one died. No one is sick. It's only some crayon—not the end of the world."

"You don't understand," I say more quietly, and as much as I try to push them away, I feel tears tickling the backs of my eyes. Mom doesn't know about the fight with Jada, about how we aren't speaking, about how I'm not even sure we're friends anymore. This scrapbook might be the last remnant of our friendship, and now it's filled with scribbles, dashed with lines and curves and unintelligible drawings.

Forever stained, just like Jada and me.

I throw the book on the floor, like a piece of trash, and I run toward the back door. Without texting her first, without even changing out of my pajamas, I storm across my backyard in the direction of Libby's, hoping her house will be the one safe haven I have left.

★15★

I stay at Libby's for the rest of the day, and aside from a call to her dad confirming I'm there, Mom doesn't contact me. At first, with me too upset to speak, Libby and I simply watch old *Non-Instrumental* episodes, content in the comfortable quiet. But the longer I sit in her living room, the more I start to feel like myself. And when Libby suggests we head to the basement to throw some plates at the ground, I am more than ready.

"Just make sure you pitch it away from you," she instructs, handing me a royal-blue one. "Nothing like blinding yourself with a shard of cheap ceramic." I hold the plate at my hip and prepare to fling it, gripping it on the side like a Frisbee. "No, no, no," she stops me. "No tossing. You have to throw it down forcefully to create the best mosaic pieces." So I raise the plate over my shoulder and then launch it onto the concrete floor, its pieces splattering the room like a burst appendix. I look at the aftermath with awe, and then I turn to Libby.

"Can I do it again?" I ask, and she claps her hands.

"It's addictive, right?" She gives me an orange one.

"It seriously is. Very therapeutic." The orange plate sails to the floor and breaks apart, creating a bright spectrum of color. As Libby and I continue to smash, I begin to unload my issues. One by one, I tell her about Mister Kitters and the scribbled scrapbook and my fight with Jada and my problems with Dad's house and Mom's defense of Asher and Amelia and just about everything in between.

And Libby, who usually has an answer for everything, listens. Truly listens. She listens like she wants to know what I have to say. She concentrates on me, rather than on how she's going to respond. And through her concerned silence, I feel heard. And I feel better. As it turns out, I don't need Libby's advice or words of encouragement or reminders that she, too, has had a bad week before. In this moment, all I need is her attention. And Libby, to her great credit, appears to understand this.

In the evening, Libby's grandmother arrives, and over dinner, I hear about the Soleils' lives, their experiences, their stories. And after hours of focusing on me, it's nice to take a back seat, and to think about something, and some people, outside my own head.

"You can sleep over if you want," Libby offers as we finish clearing the table. "You could take my bottom bunk. I'd just have to clear off . . . a few things."

"Aka the past eleven years of your life—I saw how much was piled on that mattress!" I tease her. "It's okay. I should probably go home and, you know, try and be a big girl."

"Well, I'm here if you need to run away again. I know my dad won't mind."

"Thanks," I tell her as I walk out the door. "Really. You made my day a lot better. And I promise to restock your plate supply."

"Are you kidding? I can make enough mosaics to circle the block with those pieces we created today! Come back anytime."

And as much as I would like to stay, to not have to face Mom or Asher or Amelia, I know that I can only keep them out of sight, and more or less out of mind, for so long.

I enter my house hesitantly, the same familiar feeling of dread in the pit of my stomach. Once again, it's surprisingly quiet, with only one dim light shining in the living room. As I approach, I see Mom peer around the lamp, watching me.

"So you've returned," she speaks first, the tone of her voice betraying no emotion. I glance around, searching for Asher and Amelia, but the house remains ghostly still.

"Did they leave?" I ask, not even with hopefulness, but merely out of curiosity.

"They went to sleep early. I took them to that indoor jungle gym you used to like. It wore them out."

"Oh." I sit gingerly on the edge of the recliner's cushion, not sure what to say next.

"And how was your day?" Mom asks, and I still can't tell whether or not she's mad.

"It was good," I begin, "Libby and I watched a bunch of *Non-Instrumental* episodes to get some ideas for our group."

"So the group is happening?"

I nod. "I hope so. We put up a bunch of posters and fliers on Friday, and Mrs. Nieska agreed to be our faculty advisor. Now we have to see if anyone shows up to the first meeting."

"Is Jada joining?"

"No."

Mom tilts her head, looking at me curiously. "Why not? She likes to sing."

"She's in the musical."

Mom raises her eyebrows. "Jada made the musical?"

"Yes."

"And you didn't?"

I sigh. "I couldn't go through with the audition." I decide to be honest.

"What happened?"

"I freaked out," I confess. "The spotlights were shining in my eyes and I felt like I couldn't see the edge of the stage and I just . . ." I shrug, trailing off. "I couldn't do it."

"I'm proud of you for trying," Mom says. "Even if it didn't work out. I know how hard it was for you to try after what happened." I nod. "So is Jada enjoying herself?"

I shrug again. "I guess. We're not exactly speaking right now."

Mom sits up straighter, a look of concern on her face. "You and Jada aren't speaking?"

I lean back and stare at the ceiling. "We had a fight," I begin, "yesterday, at lunch. Ever since the auditions, she's been wrapped up in her life. But when I try to do my own thing, she gets all possessive. Like only she can do something else and make new friends, and I'm supposed to sit here, waiting for her." The words pour out of me like a leaky faucet.

"So what happened?" Mom asks. "During the fight?"

"I got mad, and I . . . I guess I snapped. And then she stormed off and went to sit with the theatre people, and we haven't spoken since."

"Come here," Mom says, patting the spot on the couch next to her. Reluctantly, I stand and cross the room, collapsing onto the cushion and letting Mom pull my head onto her shoulder.

"Why didn't you tell me any of this?" she whispers, running her fingers through my hair.

I keep my eyes forward, my shoulders weighted down by Mom's arm. "I didn't feel like talking about it. Like if I didn't mention it out loud, maybe it hadn't happened. Plus . . ."

"What?"

"Asher and Amelia were here when I got home. You were busy."

Mom doesn't say anything right away, but her fingers keep combing my hair. "You know," she begins, "all friendships go through growing pains. And I've found the longer the friendship has lasted, the more changes it's going to endure. You and Jada have always been so close, but you're becoming your own people. And those people might turn out to be very different from each other. It's always good to learn to stand on your own, to do things without the other—for the two of you especially. But the trick is finding the places where your lives still intersect, the parts that remind you why you became friends in the first place."

"I don't know if that will ever happen," I tell her. "It seems like it might be over."

"You and Jada? Never. You're going through a rough patch, but you'll come back around. Why don't you contact her now? See if she wants to talk?"

I shake my head adamantly, pulling away from Mom. "I'm mad at her. Or not mad—hurt. I don't have anything to say."

"Tell her that. Explain how you're feeling, and let her explain herself too."

I drop my chin toward my chest, fidgeting with my fingers. "I'm not ready."

"Okay," she says. "Tomorrow, then. Or the next day. You two are going to come out on the other side of this. I know you are."

I push my bangs out of my eyes and tuck my hair behind my ears. "I have Libby now. So if Jada and I are never friends again, at least I have Libby."

Mom sighs quietly. "It's great that you and Libby have gotten closer. But new friends don't have to replace the old ones. You shouldn't throw away your friendship with Jada just because a new one has come along."

I lean away from Mom, burying my head in a throw pillow. "Like Dad did with me?" I say this under my breath, and when Mom doesn't reply, I'm not sure she's heard me. And I'm certainly not going to repeat it.

But then she pulls my feet onto her lap, resting her hands on my ankles. "Your dad didn't throw you away, Wylie. He loves you very much."

"He loves them more," I say softly. "I mean, I don't care. It's fine. But he does."

"He doesn't."

"You have to say that," I tell her. "You don't know

for sure. And you don't know what it's like when I go over there. How uncomfortable it is."

Mom rubs her eyes, looking exhausted. "You're right. I don't. But I do know your dad loves you. And Asher and Amelia do too."

"They won't after today."

"Of course they will. All siblings fight—it goes with the territory. And as much as you may act like they're not your 'real' brother and sister, they absolutely are. You might have a different relationship with them— different from someone like Jada, who lives with her brothers and sees them every day—but you're still their sister. The two of them fight like cats and dogs—it's only natural that every once in a while, they'll fight with you, too."

I sit up. "Do you like them?"

"I do. More than I thought I would, based on your 'charming' description of them." She pinches my big toe. "But I'm glad that *you're* my daughter."

I smile meekly. "What time are they getting picked up tomorrow?"

"Early," Mom says. "Your dad and Amy are taking an overnight flight and coming straight from the air-port, so you won't have to deal with them for long."

I nod. "I'm going to bed, then. I'll try not to wake them."

Mom gives me a good-night kiss. "Listen, you," she says, holding on to my wrist. "Next time, talk to me. If I had known what was going on with Jada, it would have explained a lot about what happened this morning. I'm always here for you—and you first. Got it?"

"Got it. Good night." I tiptoe upstairs and crawl into my unmade bed. As I snuggle into the sheets, my ear brushes against something furry and worn. I sit up and right there, perched in the middle of my pillow, is Mister Kitters. I clutch him against my chest, as if to make up for the six years we've spent apart. I want to text Jada with the news that he's returned, but I can't. Not unless I want to be the one to give in first.

So do I?

If I don't make any mention of our fight, maybe it will go away. Maybe neither of us will talk about it again, and we can move on as if nothing happened. If that was the case, I'd relent in order to put an end to this. So I snap a photo of Mister Kitters and forward it to Jada with the caption, Look who's back.

But by the following morning, Jada still hasn't replied.

★16★

The good news is that Dad and Amy pick up Asher and Amelia incredibly early on Sunday so that Mom and I can spend the rest of the weekend in peace. The bad news is that not only is Jada continuing to give me the silent treatment, but once we arrive at school on Monday, she's refusing to even look in my direction. After a full morning of being ignored, and with no idea who I will sit with in the cafeteria, I text Libby, Do you happen to have lunch next period?

I do! In the red cafeteria. Willow Oak divides its lunches between the building's two cafeterias, and while you're supposed to go to the one where you're assigned, the aides rarely check such things.

Can I meet you there? I ask.

Absolutely. Fourth table on the right at the end of the bench.

Got it.

I might have a surprise for you, Libby writes with a smiley face.

I could use one.

As soon as the end-of-period bell rings, I dart to the red cafeteria, where I find Libby waving at me frantically. I'm barely within earshot when she starts talking.

"Ta-da!" she calls out, gesturing to the person sitting across from her. "I hereby present another member of The Intermissions!" He stands, revealing himself to be shorter than Libby, with white-blond hair and rectangular glasses. He's adorable, in a little-boy sort of way.

"Hi!" I greet him. "I'm Wylie."

"Oliver," he responds. "My sister and her friend are joining the group too—that's how I found out about it."

"Wow, really? That's great!" I say. "What are their names?"

"Abigail is my sister," Oliver tells me. "Her best friend is Audrey."

"Oh, I heard about them!" I settle beside Libby. "From Mason Swenson."

"Yeah, Abigail and Mason are on Student Council together," Oliver says. "She mentioned the group to me, and then I saw Libby passing out fliers this morning. I didn't realize you two were the founders."

"We only dreamed it up last week, so it's been kind of a whirlwind," I tell him. "But hopefully, it will be fun."

"And hopefully, we'll get on *Non-Instrumental*," Libby pipes up, and I kick her under the table. "Oh, whoops!"

"*Non-Instrumental*, the TV show?" Oliver asks. "My sister watches it. Well, I may or may not watch it, too. . . ."

"It's the best show ever," Libby replies. "So where is this mysterious sister of yours? Is she in this lunch?" I smile at her gratefully for changing the subject.

"She usually goes to the blue cafeteria," Oliver says. "I'll ask if they want to come meet you guys." As he texts Abigail, I send one to Mason.

Are you still coming to The Intermissions meeting this afternoon? I ask.

Was planning on it, **he responds instantly.** Did you ever hear from the 8th graders?

No. But I'm here with one of their brothers—he's in 6th grade, and he's planning on joining too.

"They're going to try to sneak out and come to this cafeteria instead," Oliver announces, so I send Mason another text.

Not sure where you are, but there's an impromptu a cappella meeting happening in the red cafeteria if you can swing by.

Be there in a jiff, **Mason replies. And for a second, I wonder what I've been holding against him all these years, other than the fact that Jada told me to despise him. Maybe he isn't an evil, spying troublemaker. Maybe he's a regular guy trying to find his place in this school, just like the rest of us.**

Maybe it was Jada who was the mean one all along.

★17★

That afternoon, I'm the first to arrive for *The Intermissions* meeting, and I'm shaky with anticipation. I had assumed the concept of one's knees knocking was a myth, but mine are proving otherwise. What do I know about a cappella? Libby and I could watch *Non-Instrumental* until the cows came home (her words), but that doesn't mean we know what we're doing.

I jump up and down in place, hoping to steady myself. When that doesn't work, I sit on the edge of a bench, my knees jiggling up and down.

"There you are!" Libby darts into the red cafeteria like a puppy skidding on a wet floor. "I can't believe this is happening. By the way, I forgot to tell you that I asked my dad if we could borrow his fancy video camera from work to tape our segment for *Non-Instrumental*, and he said yes, so that will look a lot better than one of us recording it on our phone—"

"Whoa, whoa, whoa," I say, standing up. I thought I was wound up, but I'm nothing compared to her. "Remember, no mention of *Non-Instrumental*. Not yet. Okay?"

Before Libby can answer, Abigail and Audrey saunter in shoulder to shoulder, staring at their respective phones and whispering in what I recognize as best-friend talk. I feel a pang of jealousy, but I force myself to brush it aside.

"Hi, guys," I greet them, and Abigail and Audrey wave simultaneously without looking up from their screens. "Psst," I whisper to Libby. "Which is which again?" It's not that Abigail and Audrey are identical, but for the life of me, I can't tell them apart. Both have long, wavy hair and hazel eyes and wear preppy clothes. They smile the same and talk the same and even blink the same and they're constantly clutching their phones, which are enclosed in matching cases. At lunch, Oliver introduced them with, "This is Abigail and Audrey," which didn't help the situation one bit.

"No idea," Libby answers through clenched teeth. "Just don't call either one by name."

"It's rude to ask at this point, right?" I whisper.

"I think so," Libby answers. "Maybe Mrs. Nieska will have everyone introduce themselves, and then we can figure it out once and for all."

Mason comes bounding into the cafeteria behind Abigail/Audrey, and Oliver follows. Libby runs over to say hello to him as Mason approaches me.

"Not a bad turnout," he remarks. "I thought we may have scared those three away during lunch, and it would only be you, me, and Little House on the Prairie." He points to Libby, who is thankfully too far away to hear him.

"Hey, be nice," I scold. "Don't make me regret letting you in the group."

Mason cocks his head, a crooked smile parting his lips. "'Letting me in,' huh? I didn't realize membership was at your discretion."

"You know what I mean."

"Well, what's with the braids?" Mason asks. "Is this an everyday thing?"

"So you're a hairstylist now?" I respond, crossing

my arms in Libby's defense. My earlier good feelings toward Mason are dissipating rapidly.

"Touchy, touchy," Mason says. "I'm only suggesting that if she's your new BFF, you could talk her into a matching hairdo, like the Bobbsey Twins over there." He gestures toward Abigail and Audrey.

"The Bobbsey Twins were a boy and a girl, not two girls," a voice states, and I whirl around and find Libby behind me.

"The Bobbsey Twins are a real thing?" Mason asks. "I thought it was an expression."

"It's a book series. My grandmother has a bunch at her house, and unlike you, I've read them. So anyway, your analogy doesn't hold up." Libby puts her hands on her hips as if challenging Mason to continue, and I chuckle at her boldness.

Mason lifts up his arm and sways it back and forth through the air. "Okay, okay, I surrender," he says. "I'm officially waving the white flag."

"Could somebody give me a hand over here?" Mrs. Nieska calls from the cafeteria entrance, trying to push an upright piano through the opening.

"You found us a piano?" I ask as we jog over.

"Borrowed it," she says. "From the band practice

. If some of you take the back end and swing it around, we should be able to slide it through." Mason and I grip the front of the piano to steer, and Libby and Oliver help Mrs. Nieska push from behind. Once it's safely inside, Mrs. Nieska positions a metal folding chair next to it. "So who would like to begin?" she asks, lowering herself onto the chair with her fingers poised over the keys.

We stare at her, confused. She wants us to sing? Already? Without introductions, or ice breakers, or waiting to see if anyone else arrives?

"We're starting?" I vocalize what everyone is thinking.

"No time like the present," Mrs. Nieska says. "Don't panic—nothing too complicated. I want us to try an exercise that my college a cappella group used to do. It's a chance to hear everyone's vocal styles. No pressure— pretend you're singing in the shower and use the most natural part of your voice." The six of us shift from one foot to the other, uneasy. I had thought today would be about the formalities of starting a new group—taking down names and contact information, passing out permission slips, explaining the practice schedule, stuff like that.

Not actually, you know, *singing*. In front of one another.

"Should we wait and see if anyone else shows up?" Libby asks. "It's only a few minutes late, and—"

"If they do, they can join in. I guarantee they'll know the song," Mrs. Nicska says as she begins plunking out a melody on the piano—one I swiftly recognize as "Row, Row, Row Your Boat." "So who would like to begin?" she asks again. I look down at the floor, hoping that a lack of eye contact will signal her not to call on me.

"You don't have to raise your hand," Mrs. Nieska states, and I glance up and see Abigail/Audrey standing with their left hands, still holding their phones, in the air. "Are you volunteering?" The two of them—I swear at the same time—shake their heads no.

"We're using a piano?" one of them asks. "I thought a cappella groups weren't supposed to use instruments."

"We'll be using a piano for practicing, absolutely," she tells them. "Once again, I'll ask the question: Who would like to begin?"

"I'll do it," Mason pipes up beside me.

"Excellent," Mrs. Nieska says, standing and resting her elbows on top of the piano. "Now, don't think too much. Just sing. Sing like you're trying to entertain your baby cousin, but your cousin is way across the room. So sing out, and proudly, but in your natural voice."

Mason nods, shifting the rim of his baseball cap from one side to the other. I hear him take a breath, and then he begins, "Row, row, row your boat, gently down the stream . . ."

At the sound of his voice, my jaw drops in shock. I hastily snap it back, causing my teeth to click together, loudly enough for Libby to hear.

And to start giggling.

But she's not giggling out loud—it's the kind of laugh that happens when you're not supposed to be laughing at all. When you know you should stop, but the more you try to suppress it, the more it escapes. Her face grows redder, her shoulders rise, and her giggle comes out like a wheeze.

And as much as I try to prevent it, I start laughing too. Silently at first, but then out loud. Mason stops singing, and the entire group gawks at Libby and me. I cover my face with my hands, willing myself to stop and feeling worse the longer it goes on. Because the thing is, Libby and I aren't laughing because Mason has a bad voice. It's not nasally or gravelly or remotely off-key.

Rather, Mason's voice is beautiful. It's deep and lovely and powerful: one you would never expect to come out of his mouth.

"Sorry," Libby tries to explain. "I laugh sometimes when I get nervous. It slips out."

"So I make you nervous, eh?" Mason asks, and even without looking at him, I can tell he's smirking, proud of himself.

"You have a great voice," Libby says sincerely. "I wasn't expecting that. My voice isn't good at all."

"There's no such thing as a good voice and a bad voice in here," Mrs. Nieska says. "Some voices are stronger at certain things than others, but that's the beauty of a cappella: Everyone has a place. Now—without giggles this time, please—let's try that again. Mason, you begin. Sing the whole verse through, and when Mason reaches the 'merrily' line for the second time, someone else jump in."

"So we're singing it as a round?" Oliver asks.

"Precisely," Mrs. Nicska says. "And keep singing until everyone has joined in one by one. But again, don't think too much—don't attempt to harmonize, don't try to hit a certain key. Just sing. Like you would at home. As if no one were listening."

She points at Mason, gesturing for him to start, and he sings, "Row, row, row your boat, gently down the stream. Merrily, merrily, merrily, merrily, life is but a dream. Row, row, row your boat, gently down the stream . . ." Mrs. Nieska raises her arm for someone else to join him, and Abigail or Audrey opens her mouth. She starts the song from the beginning, and she has a pleasant, if not very distinct voice. When it's time for a new person, her second half follows, and not surprisingly, their voices are virtually indistinguishable. Oliver is next, and his voice is as high as Mason's is deep, but pretty and melodic in a way that would fit in with a prestigious all-boy choir.

This leaves only Libby and me, and she pinches the back of my arm. "I'll go first," she whispers. "I don't want to be the last one singing." On Mrs. Nieska's cue, Libby begins. And while her voice might not be the most musically inclined, she's certainly the most enthusiastic, swinging her arms back and forth to the beat.

As she reaches the end of the first verse, I clear my throat and close my eyes. Forcing myself not to over-think, I open my mouth and sing. I hear my voice ring out across the cafeteria, blending in with those around me, obscured but still somehow my own all at the same time.

★18★

The six members of The Intermissions gather the following day at the same lunch table, settling down comfortably as if we've eaten this way forever, and I realize that it's the first time I've ever shared lunch with a group—*my group*—of people.

"What are you smiling at?" Mason catches me, and I swiftly lower the corners of my lips.

"Nothing," I answer.

"It had to have been something," he says, pulling at the top of his miniature milk carton.

"Chocolate milk, huh?" I ask, attempting to distract him. "The kindergarteners called and they want their snack back."

"I like to keep myself youthful," he replies, prying two of the carton's corners apart harshly and splashing milk over his chicken nuggets in the process.

"Oh no, save them!" I call, throwing my napkin onto his tray while Mason watches.

"I never realized you were so attached to nuggets," he says, lifting the soggy napkin off his food. "Plus, chocolate milk sounds like a pretty great condiment to me." He makes a big display of dipping one into the brown puddle. "Mmmmm."

"Ewwwww," Abigail and Audrey call out simultaneously, which only encourages him.

I glance over at Libby, who looks less than amused by Mason's antics. She leans toward me and whispers, "We should tell them about the contest."

"Not now," I reply, as the volume around us grows, forcing us to raise our voices.

"Everyone needs to be on the same page," Libby insists. "We have to tell them."

"Tell them what?" Mason asks, and our table falls suddenly quiet.

"It's nothing," I maintain.

"It's *not* nothing," Libby says. "It's exciting."

"What's exciting? What are you talking about? What's the secret? What are you keeping from us?" The rest of The Intermissions begin speaking at once, and I raise my hand to stop them.

"Okay, fine. Do you want to do the honors, or should I?" I ask Libby.

"You can do it," Libby says, drumming her fingers against the table to build suspense.

"So you know *Non-Instrumental*?" I ask.

"The TV show?" Audrey (I think) clarifies.

"Yes," I say. "They're holding a contest for a cappella groups from around the country." I look at Libby to continue.

"Those chosen will be featured in a promo piece for the show. Annnnnnnd . . ." She drags out the final word, gesturing for me to fill in the blanks.

"The winning groups get a video call with Colby Cash. You know, from Marquis Machine?" I explain.

"The one you have plastered all over your locker?" Mason asks.

"Well, yes," I say. "He's hosting the show this season and—"

"So you're using us as your means to Colby, eh?" Mason asks with a smirk. "And here I thought your a cappella intentions were so pure."

"To be fair, Libby and I dreamed this up *before* we found out about the contest," I defend myself. "The Colby piece is a bonus."

"Sure it is," Mason says in a singsong voice. "So what do you want us to do to win you a call?"

"That's the thing," I begin, "if we want to enter the contest, our timeline becomes much more urgent."

"What's urgent?" Abigail (maybe?) asks. "I mean, I love *Non-Instrumental*. I'd like to get featured on it if we can. But what kind of timeline are we looking at?"

I turn to Libby, and she answers, "The deadline for submitting an audition video is next Thursday. So—"

"Next Thursday?!" Abigail or Audrey interrupts her. "How is that even possible?"

"I guess they figure that most groups who will enter are already established," Libby says, "and they won't need that much time to prepare."

"What would we even sing?" Mason asks. "Because I don't think 'Row, Row, Row Your Boat' is going to cut it."

"We only need to learn one song," I tell them. "That's doable, right?" But even as I say it, my tone sounds as skeptical as the group's faces look.

"We could totally do that," Libby pipes up. "Come on, guys. What's the harm in trying?"

I see Abigail and Audrey exchange a doubtful glance, and I recognize how crazy our plan must sound. "Listen, if you don't want to—" I begin, but Oliver stops me.

"I agree with Libby. We should try. This is our chance to get on TV!"

"But we only have one more rehearsal scheduled before next Thursday," Mason points out.

"Then we practice more," Libby says. "Every day if we have to."

"Exactly," Oliver concurs. "We can even practice this weekend. Right, Abigail?" I snap my head so fast to see which one replies that I nearly give myself whiplash.

Abigail and Audrey look at each other again, as if asking permission to answer, before Abigail (finally! I know for sure!) replies, "My brother's right. We should give it a shot. Mrs. Nieska can help us."

"She doesn't know about the contest yet," I reveal. "But I can talk to her about it today, if we're ready to move forward. So . . . are we?"

"Let's take a vote," Libby suggests. "All in favor say 'Colby Cash!'"

"Um, can we say something else?" Mason whines. "I don't want to ruin my street cred."

"You have street cred?" I cock my head at him.

"All in favor," Mason begins with a grin, "say 'Here goes nothing.'"

"Such a pessimist," I whisper jokingly, as on a count of three, we all call out a resounding "Here goes nothing!" Libby bursts into animated applause.

"Great," I say. "I'll speak to Mrs. Nieska. It's probably too late to set up a practice for today, but let's plan on having daily after-school rehearsals starting tomorrow?"

Everyone nods as the end-of-lunch bell rings, and Mason dips his last nugget into the chocolate milk with a flourish.

"You're kind of gross, you know that?" I ask him as I clean up.

"I kind of do," he says, and I shake my head, smiling.

Libby pulls on my wrist. "Text me how it goes with Mrs. Nieska."

"I will."

"Want to watch last night's *Non-Instrumental* with me tonight?" she asks.

"You haven't watched yet? I *did* think it was strange that you weren't texting me every fifteen seconds during Staccato Skaters' performance."

"Hey, no spoilers!" she yells.

"Well, I'm always up for a repeat Colby viewing. Tell me when you want to come over."

"Will do!" Libby calls as she skips toward the door. "Toodle-oo!"

"Who says that?" I shout after her.

"Me and seventy-seven-year-old women!"

As I make my way into the hallway, my head swims with thoughts about the contest: What if we *did* win? Would Jada really let me call Colby Cash without her? Never. She would insist on joining, on "meeting" him at the same time. Which means that winning could be the way to bring us back together, to break the tension that has fallen between us. Winning could repair everything.

So how could The Intermissions give ourselves the best chance? What song could we learn—and perfect—in one week? Should I ask Mom if the group can come to our house this weekend?

This weekend—wait a minute. This is the "other" weekend—the "every other weekend" that I have to go to Dad's. I had almost forgotten, since I just saw Asher and Amelia. Could I get out of it?

I walk into Social Studies and spot Jada across the room, her face turned toward the window, spitefully making sure we don't make eye contact. And while I try not to let it bother me, just for a second, it does.

Maybe even for more than a second.

★ 19 ★

Thankfully, Mrs. Nieska is fully on board with participating in the contest: She thinks that working toward a common goal is the perfect way to help band the group together—even if it does mean practicing every day.

Including the weekend.

I decide that if there's any way I'm going to get out of going to Dad's, I'll need Mom's support. She has to understand that this isn't about me avoiding Asher and Amelia, but that it's for the good of The Intermissions, and therefore it isn't really about *me* at all. I have to convince her of this so she can plead my case with Dad, especially since, as far as I'm concerned, he owes her after last weekend.

"Hi," I greet Mom when she trudges in after work, looking more tired than usual. "What would you like for dinner? I'll help make it."

Mom looks me up and down. "What are you up to?"

"What do you mean?" I ask innocently.

"Wylie. I know you better than anyone—better, sometimes, than you know yourself. And if you're volunteering for something, it means you're looking for a favor. Spill it."

I drop my perky demeanor and rest my palms on the counter. "I can't go to Dad's this weekend. My a cappella group has to practice, so I need your help getting out of it."

Mom slides her jacket off. "That's between you and your father," she tells me slowly. "But this wouldn't have anything to do with last weekend, would it?"

"No, I promise." I shake my head adamantly. "We *need* to practice. There's this contest on *Non-Instrumental* that we want to enter, but we barely have a week to pull together a submission video. So we want to meet every day, including this weekend."

"I understand the conflict, but you made a commitment to your dad."

"*I* didn't make the commitment," I insist. "The commitment was made for me. And it was made before I was in middle school with my own life and friends and activities *here*."

Mom gives me an enormous sigh. "As I've told you, I know the setup isn't ideal. But someday, you're going to be glad that your dad and Asher and Amelia and Amy are in your life. At least, that's my hope. So now, as hard as it is at times, I think you have to follow through. But like I said—you can take this up with your father."

"Ugh," I groan, retrieving my phone and heading toward the stairs.

"So no more helping with dinner?" Mom yells after me.

"I have to call Dad!" But when I get to my room, I do anything I can to avoid calling Dad. I browse my phone, I rearrange my bookshelf, I straighten the Colby posters on my wall, I even read an extra chapter of our assigned reading, all to put off the conversation. I procrastinate so long that I still haven't placed the call by the time we sit down for dinner. And Mom, to her credit, doesn't ask about it.

But she does ask about Jada.

"Nothing's changed. We're not speaking," I explain curtly.

"Not at all?" Mom asks, mixing the food around on her plate.

"It's fine," I say. "It is what it is."

"It's not fine, Wy," Mom says. "I can tell by your face that it's not fine. And no amount of a cappella is going to make up for that."

"I thought you wanted me to try new things."

"I do," she says. "And I'm proud of you for the initiative you've taken—for becoming a leader in this group. But that doesn't mean you and Jada can't be friends anymore. Friends can have different interests and different activities. That's normal for growth and—"

"Can we please not talk about this anymore?" I ask quietly. "You've told me all this. But I can't fix it. Not right now, anyway."

"Okay," Mom says. "I won't bring it up again—as long as you promise to come to me when you're ready to talk about it."

"I will."

"So what's the deal with this contest?" I fill her in on the details, on the Colby-related prize, on the members of The Intermissions, on what we've done so far and what we need to accomplish before next Thursday. And once dinner is finished, I text Libby and tell her she can come over whenever she's ready for our *Non-Instrumental* viewing.

She arrives minutes later, and we settle on the couch, our eyes glued to the screen. But soon after Colby's introduction, my phone begins ringing in my pocket. I pull it out and look at the screen.

Jada.

I think about not answering. About playing hard to get. About making Jada grovel for my forgiveness. But my curiosity—and truthfully, my relief at hearing from her—wins out, and I hightail it toward my room, calling, "Be right back!" over my shoulder.

"Hello?" I answer tentatively, but I only hear loud breathing. Is this some kind of prank? "Hello?" I repeat, more hostile this time.

"Wylie?" Jada's voice. Only it sounds different. Faraway and sort of weak.

"Yeah?" I respond, not sure about her intentions. Is she with her new theatre people friends? Is this some sort of setup?

"It's me," Jada says, as if I don't know. But with those two words, Jada betrays something else: tears. I hear them in her voice.

"What's wrong?" I ask immediately.

"I miss you. And . . . and," she stammers. "And I really need my best friend right now."

"What's wrong?" I repeat. "What happened?"

"It's the musical." She gasps for breath, trying to regain composure. "I lost my part."

"What do you mean? Like the script?"

"No, the role itself," Jada says. "I'm not playing Tallulah anymore."

"Why not?"

"It's a long story," she begins. "Tallulah has a big tap dance number at the end of the first act. And I couldn't get it. I tried and I tried and I practiced and I practiced—all week, constantly—and I was still terrible."

"So you quit?" I ask, and a part of me—the part that is mad at Jada—feels like gloating. But the other part—the part that is still Jada's friend—hates to hear her so upset.

"No, they assigned me a different part. In the chorus."

"So that's good, right?" I ask. "It's not like you got kicked out entirely."

"I have three lines in the entire show!" Jada whines. "And not a single song. What's the point of being in a musical without any music?"

"But you're *in* the show. Isn't that what you wanted?"

"I don't know. Without getting to sing, it's not that fun anymore. I kind of want to . . . stop." I climb onto my bed and prop myself up with pillows, sensing this conversation isn't going to end quickly. "I didn't expect it to be so hard."

"Then leave," I suggest. "You shouldn't do something that makes you miserable. It's not worth it."

"I sort of want to. But I also don't want to look like a quitter, like I couldn't handle it. I'd probably be banned from future shows, and what if I want to try out for the spring musical?"

"Then don't quit. Not exactly," I say. "Offer your role to someone else. Are there others who would want it?"

"Definitely. They cut a ton of people at the auditions."

"Then say you'd like to give another person the opportunity to be in the show," I begin, "because you're joining a different musical group: The Intermissions." I blurt out the idea before giving myself time to consider it.

"A cappella?" Jada asks. "I've never done a cappella."

"Neither have any of the rest of us. That's the beauty of it," I tell her. "Come on. You wouldn't want me to get to speak to Colby without you, would you?"

"What are you talking about?" Jada asks suspiciously, and I tell her about the contest, convinced that this is the perfect plan for getting us back on track. Because if Jada joins The Intermissions, it would mean that our friendship has returned to normal, that things haven't changed, that this week has been a fluke, that we're best friends again and always will be.

That is, I sincerely hope that's what it would mean.

★20★

After I hang up the phone, I practically skip back to the living room, the relief of Jada and me being on speaking terms lightening my gait.

"Sorry about that," I say, flopping down beside Libby. "Jada was having a crisis."

"So you two are friends again?"

"It seems that way. Fingers crossed. Did you see the Staccato Skaters?"

"Yeah, they were good," Libby replies glumly, rising from the couch. "I better get home."

"But there are still twenty minutes left," I point out. "And you haven't seen Colby's closing number."

"I'll watch it later," Libby says as my phone dings with a text. I look down and find a message from Jada: Is Mason still in the group?

Yes, I answer. But he's been on his best behavior. Seriously. And believe it or not, he has a nice voice.

And you really think we can get on TV?

You mean win a call with COLBY CASH? I reply. Hello, priorities! We've been waiting our whole lives to talk to him! Jada doesn't respond right away, and I stare at my screen expectantly. Well? What's the verdict?

Okay, she finally answers. I think I want to do it.

Leave the musical?

And join The Intermissions. Can we talk more about it at lunch?

Sure, I say. The group has started eating together in the red cafeteria, so you can join us.

No, just you and me, Jada says. In our regular spot. I need some quality Wylie time.

Okay, I respond with a smiley face. I'm glad we're back to normal again.

Me too. See you tomorrow.

I place my phone on the couch, grinning with satisfaction. "Libby?" I call.

"I heard her leave!" Mom answers from upstairs.

"Okay." I settle back and fast-forward to Colby's song, feeling more content than I have in days. And it's not until later that night, right when I'm about to fall asleep, that I realize I completely forgot to call Dad.

Jada stands at our locker bank before Wednesday afternoon's rehearsal, jittery like a caffeinated poodle. "I did it. I resigned from the musical. I can't believe it. What if it was a mistake? Do you know how many people would kill to be in the musical? Do you realize the number of people they cut? What if this was my one chance, and I blew it?"

"Whoa, whoa, whoa." I hold up my hands like a human stop sign. "Remember: You wanted to join the musical to sing—they weren't going to let you sing."

"Yes, but maybe I should have suffered through it." Jada begins chewing on the side of her thumb, twitchy with worry. "I still would have been in the show itself, and—"

"Jada." I stop her again. "You're a fantastic singer. You're probably the best singer I know. Well, besides Colby, obviously." I pet one of the head shots in my locker.

"Obviously," Jada echoes, looking slightly more still.

"In The Intermissions, you can sing. Which is what you wanted to do in the first place, correct?" I shut my locker and we begin making our way toward the red cafeteria.

"Yes," Jada says thoughtfully. "The other members, are they good singers? I know you are, but how about the rest? Will they be better than me?"

"No," I tell her defiantly, recognizing that she requires a boost of confidence. "You'll be one of the best, without question. Possibly even *the* best."

"Okay, good," Jada says as we enter. "That's what I needed to hear." She walks away to deposit her bags on a table.

"You didn't answer my text." Libby confronts me, blocking my path. "What happened to you at lunch?"

"Sorry. I was with Jada. I meant to tell you."

"Wait, is she joining the group?" Mason appears beside us, motioning in Jada's direction.

"I thought she was in the musical," Libby adds.

"She quit—sorry, resigned from—the musical," I say, and then I turn to Mason. "No funny business. I'm begging you."

"I can't make any promises," he tells me with his typical smirk, and we assemble in front of the piano, Libby on one side of me and Mason on the other. Jada marches up and gives Mason a glaring once-over before stepping into the narrow space between Libby and me.

"Jada," Mrs. Nieska begins, "I didn't realize you'd be joining us. Welcome."

"Thank you," Jada says as those to our left shift over to make room.

"I assume you know about the tight deadline we're under?" Mrs. Nieska asks. "With the *Non-Instrumental* contest?"

"Yes, I heard from Wylie," Jada answers. "She'll stop at nothing to get Colby Cash's attention." She laughs at her own remark as some of the others snicker, and I feel my face redden. I look down at the floor, trying to push aside the mocking tone I heard in Jada's voice.

"Okay, then," Mrs. Nieska begins, hitting a deafening chord on the piano. "What would you say is the most important aspect of any successful a cappella group?" She looks at each of us one by one. "Yes, Oliver?"

"Working together?" he guesses.

"Nope. Audrey?"

"Finding the correct harmonies?"

"Nah. Mason?"

"General musicianship?"

"No," Mrs. Nieska declares. "All of those are vital, yes. But the most important aspect of a cappella—really, of any singing—is breathing." She comes around the piano so that she's standing in the center of us. "And just like anything, to become a more successful breather, you need to practice. So, breathing exercises." She lifts her arms as if conducting an orchestra. "Watch me carefully. When I expand my arms out to the sides, that's your cue to take a breath. When I bring them back to the middle, release that breath through your mouth. Let's try." Slowly, she pushes her arms out on either side, and the seven of us take deep breaths.

"Now hold it," Mrs. Nieska calls, "until I bring my arms back to the center." Silence fills the cafeteria, our lungs struggling not to breathe, until Mason lets out a sputtering belch, causing a domino effect of cascading laughter.

"Sorry, sorry," he says. "I swear that wasn't on purpose."

"Yeah, right," Jada jeers, the only one, including Mrs. Nieska, who doesn't look remotely amused by Mason's accidental outburst.

"Let's try again," Mrs. Nieska instructs once we've calmed down, and she extends her arms out. Without incident this time, we hold our collective breath until she collapses them at her sides, signaling us to release. "Excellent," she says. "Now let's do it again, and make sure you're paying attention—I'm going to vary how long you have to hold it." We go through the exercise multiple times, at faster paces, slower paces, with shorter breaths and longer breaths. Until the seven members of The Intermissions are eventually breathing as one.

"So are we actually going to sing today?" Jada asks as we walk to Thursday's rehearsal. "There's only so long I can learn to breathe."

"We sang yesterday," I remind her.

"One note at a time so we could follow Mrs. Nieska's hand movements? I wouldn't exactly call that singing. I literally did more in the musical, and I was cut from every song."

"We have to start somewhere," I say defensively.

"And Mrs. Nieska knows what she's doing—she did a cappella in college."

"Yeah, but that was decades ago," Jada says. "I don't think 1980s college a cappella is the same as *Non-Instrumental* national television a cappella."

"Shhh." I shush her as we enter the red cafeteria. "I think she's doing a great job."

"We have—what?—one week left to pull together a video?" Jada asks. "Do you truly think you're going to get your Colby call by learning how to breathe for two hours?" With that, she gallops ahead to the piano and asks Mrs. Nieska, "So are we going to sing a song today?"

"Perhaps," Mrs. Nieska answers. "One step at a time. But speaking of which, I'd like to hear your voice on its own to get an idea of your style. I had a chance to experience everyone else's on the first day."

"Sure. What do you want me to sing?" Jada asks, and I settle onto a bench as the rest of the group filters in. "I could do 'Somewhere Over the Rainbow,' or a song from *Wicked*—'Defying Gravity,' maybe?"

"'Row, Row, Row Your Boat,'" Mrs. Nieska answers. "Like everyone else did."

"Seriously?" Jada asks.

"Serious as a heart attack," Mrs. Nieska answers, and I hear Mason snort. "But follow my conducting. Stay on my rhythm." She raises her arms to guide Jada, expanding them to signal that Jada should take a breath. Jada does so obediently, and when Mrs. Nieska begins waving her arms down, in, out, and up, cueing the beats of the song, Jada sings, "Row, row, row your boat . . . ," following Mrs. Nieska perfectly. Her tone is strong, dynamic, and a tad higher than mine. She has an excellent voice, definitely. She always has.

And from the way she's singing—shoulders back, chin in the air, feet square on the ground—I get an uneasy feeling that she knows it, that the insecurity she expressed only yesterday has vanished, replaced by an overt confidence.

The confidence of a solo artist in a room full of people meant to sing as one.

★21★

"Okay, I need some volunteers," Mrs. Nieska announces later during rehearsal while distributing lyric sheets. "Who wants to take the first line?" Jada shoots her hand in the air, but Mrs. Nieska calls on Mason. "Mason, terrific. I think you'll be perfect to start this off." We have just listened to the song Mrs. Nieska chose for us—"Somebody to Love"—three times so we could get a sense of the melody. "Now look," she continues. "Think of this as an experiment. I expect it to be a mess today, tomorrow, maybe even after that. But if we stick with it, and we focus specifically on this song, I believe we will nail a performance successful enough to submit to *Non-Instrumental*."

"So this is the song we're singing?" Jada asks. "Is that definite?"

"We decided at lunch that Mrs. Nieska should choose our song," Audrey says, testiness in her voice. "You two weren't there." Her eyes pinball between Jada and me.

"Right. Mrs. Nieska is the a cappella expert here," Abigail adds, glancing at her phone as if bored by the discussion. "Not you," she adds under her breath.

"I was *just asking*," Jada says, crossing her arms, haughty. "You don't have to jump all over me." I see Abigail and Audrey exchange a look.

A look that is definitely not Jada-friendly.

"To answer your question, I wouldn't say it's the final decision," Mrs. Nieska says. "But the sooner we make a choice, the better. One week doesn't give us time to keep switching."

"I think we should do 'Somebody to Love,'" Libby pipes up. "We're wasting time debating it." Oliver, Abigail, and Audrey nod their agreement.

"Okay, then," Mrs. Nieska begins, "Mason, since you're going to sing the first line by yourself, why don't you stand in the center of the group?" Mason steps between Jada and me as Jada grimaces. "Now, do you remember the lyric?"

"Can anybody find me . . . ," Mason sings, his voice strong, ringing out across the cafeteria. Mrs. Nieska cuts him off.

"Excellent, Mason," she says, and I catch Jada rolling her eyes. "Now the rest of you are going to join him on the words 'somebody to love.' Again, sing as naturally as possible. Don't try to harmonize or do anything fancy. We can tweak later." She cues Mason to sing the line again, and then we all join in tentatively. Mrs. Nieska stops us. "Remember, this is your first impression. You don't want *Non-Instrumental* to pause your video before you've gotten started!" We sing the line again, and then once more. Mrs. Nieska walks in front of us, listening. She rearranges our order, placing me on one end of the semicircle, and Jada on the opposite side next to Libby. And after our ninth run-through of that single phrase, she applauds, exclaiming, "Masterful! Give yourselves a pat on the back!"

"Is this next part a solo?" Jada interrupts the collective congratulations, pointing to the lyrics. "If so, can I take it?"

A hush falls over the room, and without anyone saying a word, I can feel it: annoyed exasperation. Directed at Jada.

"There's no set rule when it comes to solos," Mrs. Nieska explains. "Everyone who wants one can have one—it's only a matter of figuring out where voices fit best."

"Everyone is going to have a solo?" Jada asks, and if I weren't standing so far away, I would be doing whatever it takes to quiet her.

"Anyone who wants one, yes," Mrs. Nieska answers. "We certainly won't force anyone who's not comfortable."

"But shouldn't the solos go to the strongest voices?" Jada asks, and I open my eyes wide, staring at her, willing her to stop, but she never looks at me. "Wouldn't that give us a better chance of winning?"

"I won't take a solo," Libby interjects, hostility in her tone, "if that's what you're so worried about."

"I didn't say . . ." Jada tries to defend herself, but the room has turned against her. "It wasn't a personal dig against anyone specifically. I was *just asking*."

"Libby *should* have a solo," Oliver pipes up. "She's the most fun performer of any of us."

"I don't need a solo," Libby says. "Unlike some people, I don't always need to be the center of attention." She glares at Jada, and I see Jada's eyebrows pucker. "Just because you got kicked out of the musical doesn't mean you can come here and take over."

"Libby, that's enough," Mrs. Nieska says, but Libby is on a roll.

"You're no better than the rest of us," she adds.

"And you're throwing off the whole dynamic." Abigail backs her up. "This isn't even your group. Wylie and Libby are the ones who started it."

"Abigail, Libby, I've asked you to—" Mrs. Nieska begins, but before she can continue, Jada marches away from the semicircle and storms out of the cafeteria. And if nothing else, I'm certain of one thing: In Jada's mind, this is going to end up being my fault.

Though we had tried to continue our rehearsal, we all seemed rattled by Jada's departure and ended up finishing early. With The Intermissions now more desperate for practice time than ever, that night I lock myself in my room and call Dad to ask about skipping the visit this weekend, but he refuses. A few minutes after I hang up, a soft knock sounds on my door.

I call out to Mom, "I don't want to talk about it," but she comes in anyway.

"Your dad said no?" she asks.

"Of course he did. Because no one ever cares what I want." I pout.

"You know that's not true. You explained the situation? About your group?"

"I tried to, but he cut me off because Amelia was throwing a fit in the background. He said, 'We need to stick to the schedule,' and that was the end."

Mom sits on the edge of my bed. "I'm sorry, Wy. I know you often feel caught in the middle."

"That might as well be my middle name," I tell her.

"What might?"

"Caught-in-the-middle," I say.

"Things are still dicey with Jada?" she asks.

"They were better for like a day. And now . . ." I trail off. "She joined The Intermissions, but she was being kind of bossy and the rest of the group started to push back on her. And then she quit. At least, I think she quit. I haven't heard from her since."

"What happened to the musical?" Mom asks.

"She quit that, too. I felt bad, so I invited her to join The Intermissions, which was clearly a mistake."

Mom sighs. "Do you want me to make hot chocolate? We can sit on the couch and—"

"I'd rather this day just be over with," I tell her, and Mom nods.

"Okay." She leans over and kisses my forehead. "Sleep tight. Things are bound to look brighter in the morning." She turns off the light as she closes the door, and I slink down in bed, throwing a pillow over my face, blocking out the world.

But unfortunately not blocking out the sound of my phone, which starts buzzing incessantly. I reach toward my nightstand.

Thanks for your support today. Really grateful to you for having my back. Jada.

I groan out loud and throw my phone toward my feet, pulling the covers over my head and squinting my eyes closed, and after what feels like hours, I fall into a fitful sleep.

The moment I spot Abigail and Audrey standing at my locker the next morning, I'm filled with dread. Are they about to quit The Intermissions too?

"Hey, so I know yesterday's practice didn't go as well as we hoped, but I think—" I begin before Abigail cuts me off.

"Did you hear?" she asks. "Did you hear what she's doing?"

"Who?"

"Jada," Audrey answers, holding up her phone,

which displays a selfie of six faces crowding into the frame. "She's starting her own group. She and some of the theatre people. One of them posted about it this morning."

"What kind of group?" I ask, dumbfounded. "An a cappella group?"

"Yes, an a cappella group," a voice responds behind me: Jada herself, twisting her locker combination. "One where all members are appreciated—and not scorned like outsiders."

"We would have welcomed you if you had been a little humbler," Abigail tells her.

"Jada," I say quietly, wishing Abigail and Audrey would go away so we could speak privately. Alone, I could reason with Jada. This isn't the first time I've seen her react too strongly to something, to let her temper flare out of control: Mason knocked her off a seesaw, and she declared him her lifelong nemesis; she was told she wasn't a great tap dancer, and she resigned from the musical; she had one bad rehearsal with The Intermissions, and she ran off and started her own group. This is Jada's pattern; it isn't a good one, but it's hers.

"Anything you want to say to me, you should have said yesterday," Jada tells me, her voice calm and cold.

"You know, during that time when you should have stood up for me." With that, she slams her locker and marches into homeroom, leaving us in her dust.

I push my bangs back, thinking. "There's no way Jada was able to pull a whole group together—plus find a faculty advisor—in one night," I reason.

"They found a faculty advisor—the choral teacher," Audrey says. The homeroom bell rings then, warning us to wrap things up.

"I'll talk to Mrs. Nieska," I tell them. "I'll let you know at lunch what she says." Once they're gone, I head inside and over to Jada's desk. "Why are you doing this?" I ask. "You're making a big deal out of nothing."

"It's not nothing to me," Jada says, refusing to match my gaze. "I left the musical to join *your* group, and I was ganged up on."

"No one ganged up on you," I say impatiently. "You're being dramatic. As usual."

"Wow." Jada crosses her arms and leans back in her chair, raising her eyes and glaring at me full-on. "Why don't you say how you really feel?"

"You never even cared about a cappella," I point out.

"Neither did you."

"But Colby—"

"Exactly. The only reason you're doing this silly group is to try to get face time with Colby Cash. It's sad is what it is." My eyes widen with shock. "Some of us actually care about our musicianship." Without responding, I turn on my heel and stomp to our homeroom teacher's desk to ask if I can go to Mrs. Nieska's classroom, and then I hurry down the seventh-grade wing.

"I heard," Mrs. Nieska says as soon as she sees me. "But it's not the end of the world." And even though her words may be accurate, she can't persuade me into believing them.

"You're joining us again?" Mason asks as I take a seat at The Intermissions' cafeteria table.

"I would certainly hope so," Abigail says, "after what Jada did."

"Did you speak to Mrs. Nieska?" Audrey asks.

"Yeah," I say. "She thinks we should carry on with our plans and forget about Jada's group."

"We can't," Libby says quietly, looking down at the tabletop.

"Sure we can," Oliver tells her. "It's an irritation, but it doesn't affect us."

"It does," Libby says. "Only one a cappella group

per organization can enter the contest. According to the rules."

"What does that mean?" Oliver asks. "We both can't enter, or we both can't win? If we both can't win, then I guess that makes sense. But if we can't enter—"

"If more than one group enters from a single organization, like a school, both will be disqualified," Libby states, as if reading from a manual. "So if Jada's group enters, she'll automatically kick us out."

"But she'd kick herself out too," Audrey says. "She wouldn't be able to win."

"Yes," Libby agrees. "But that doesn't help us."

"So much for you wooing Colby Cash," Mason says, and I kick him under the table.

"Can't someone talk to her?" Oliver asks. "This seems like a lot to do about nothing."

"Wylie?" Abigail suggests.

I shake my head. "Jada's not exactly being reasonable right now."

"I have a whole slew of pranks I haven't tried yet," Mason volunteers. "Maybe it's time to unleash the peanut butter cup/banana peel/crusty toothpaste surprise to throw her off her game."

I smile despite myself. "I feel like that would only end

up getting *us* in trouble, which wouldn't help the cause."

"But we can't give up yet," Oliver says. "We have this whole weekend to practice. We can get together all day, every day if we need to. And maybe in the meantime, Mrs. Nieska will work things out with the chorus teacher and put an end to this nonsense."

"I can't practice this weekend," I blurt out.

"I thought we had agreed that we would," Abigail says.

"I know, I'm sorry. I tried, but . . ." I don't finish.

"Are you joining Jada's group?" Libby asks, looking accusatory.

"What? No!"

"But you might," Libby carries on, her eyes narrowed. "If Jada walked over right now and begged you to join her group, you would."

"I would not!" I yell back, shocked by Libby's tone.

"Whatever," she says, rising from the bench and throwing the remainder of her lunch in the trash. She trudges away, and I hurry to catch her, grabbing her by the elbow as she reaches the exit.

"Hey!" I call, but she pulls out of my grasp, jogging across the hall and into the girls' bathroom. I follow her inside, but she has already barricaded herself in the largest stall. "Hey!" I call again. "What's wrong? Why are you acting like this?" Libby doesn't answer, and I peer underneath the other four stalls, making sure they're empty. "Libby. Talk to me."

After a few endless seconds, her stall door swings open, and I find Libby leaning against the wall, arms crossed and a scowl on her face.

"What is it?" I ask, looking her up and down, trying to figure out what could possibly have made her so angry at me, and so quickly.

"You really have no idea?" she asks, and her voice catches on the last word, signaling that she's about to cry.

"Hey," I say more gently, joining her inside and closing the door. "Please talk to me."

I lean against the partition and wait for her to respond. For a moment, I'm afraid she's going to ignore me, to run out and stop speaking to me completely, just like Jada. But then she says, more quietly than I've ever heard Libby speak, "I'm always second choice."

"Huh? What do you mean?"

Libby takes a deep breath before facing me. "It's like I'm your backup friend," she explains. "You only want to hang out with me when you and Jada are fighting. But the second you two make up, I disappear."

I shake my head. "That's not what—" I begin, but Libby cuts me off.

"It's how you make me feel. Whether you mean to or not. I'm like the leftovers."

"You're not," I promise her. "I'm sorry I made you feel like that. I truly am."

"But if Jada walked in right now, and she apologized to you, you'd walk out with her," Libby says, not even angry anymore, but sad. "I know this isn't your fault, but I've never had a best friend before. Not like you and Jada have always had each other. I'm not trying to be your new best friend, but . . ."

"You felt like a replacement," I fill in. "I'm sorry."

"Okay," Libby says, and after a beat, she continues, "And I'm sorry I blew up back there in front of everyone." She unrolls some toilet paper and blows her nose before offering the wad to me. "Want some snotty tissue?" she asks, which makes us both laugh, breaking the tension.

"Let's promise each other one thing," I tell her, unlocking the stall door. "No more heart-to-hearts over a school toilet."

"Or over *any* toilet would be even better."

"Good point," I tell her, pausing as we reach the

sinks. I catch her eye in the mirror's reflection. "I really am sorry. I hope you know that. And I'm so glad we're friends."

"I am too," Libby says. "But you know what would make me gladder?"

"What?"

"Winning!" she exclaims, skipping toward the bathroom door. "Now hurry up—we need a game plan, and fast!" I run after her, and though I'm relieved that we're back on track, I can't help but think that in less than a week, I've nearly lost not one friend, but two.

Which means that maybe it isn't my friends' behavior at all. Maybe it's mine. I'm the common denominator of the fights this week. Maybe I have to stop blaming everyone else for what's going wrong and start taking responsibility for myself.

But then I step into the hall, and there in front of me is a glittery poster proclaiming, THE OVERTURES: WILLOW OAK'S HOTTEST A CAPPELLA GROUP!

And in a snap, I decide that in this particular case, the blame lies squarely with none other than Jada Emmett.

★23★

By the time we leave school for the weekend, *The Intermissions* are more stressed than ever. The motivation that we had earlier in the week has vanished, and our *Non-Instrumental* goal hardly seems worth it anymore. We have less than a week left—we're never going to pull it together. And even if we do, we aren't going to win. I'm never going to get a call with Colby. We aren't going to make the promo spot. It's over. It's impossible.

And it's my fault. I'm the one who encouraged Jada to join The Intermissions, which means I'm responsible for her turning around and betraying us. And I have no idea how to fix it.

By Saturday, the last place I feel like being is Dad's, with Asher and Amelia tearing around, whining at full volume, and Dad constantly suggesting some sort of "family entertainment" (which I shoot down each time). If he insists I come here, I will come.

But I don't have to act happy about it.

Thankfully, Amy eventually shoos Asher and Amelia outside with their scooters, but their voices float through the window as they fight over who's winning. I lift a throw pillow and smash it against my face, silencing a groan.

"Scooters weren't such a big thing when you were their age, huh?" I hear Dad's voice, and I lower the pillow to my lap.

"I never had one," I answer shortly, pretending to be suddenly fascinated by my phone.

Not taking the hint, Dad settles on the other end of the couch, and I instinctively lean in the opposite direction, as if distancing myself from whatever conversation is about to take place.

"So," he begins, sounding almost as uncomfortable as I feel. "Your mom said we should talk." I squint, simultaneously annoyed with Mom for forcing this exchange on me, and irritated with Dad for needing Mom to instruct him to speak to me. "She said this setup is getting hard for you, now that you're older," Dad continues. "Having to leave your activities and come here every other weekend. Is that true?"

I nod, fearing that I'm walking into a trap. "I don't like having to drop everything," I explain, trying not to sound angry. "I have to miss a lot."

"Like what? Birthday parties and stuff?"

"Sometimes, but that's always been the case. It's more the big things. Like this weekend, I needed to be home. And you wouldn't listen to me."

"I'm listening now," Dad says, his eyes gentle, open. Listening.

"It's just, with my a cappella group—we had a rough week. We're on a deadline, and we needed to rehearse this weekend. And with me here, we can't. So the whole group is in limbo."

"You're in an a cappella group? I didn't know that."

"My friend and I started it. There are only six of us, so if one person is missing, it's a big deal."

"And what's this deadline you're referring to?" Dad asks.

"The TV show *Non-Instrumental*—they're having a

contest. But the last day to submit a video is Thursday, and we're definitely not ready. Though that may not even matter anymore, because we might be disqualified."

"Why's that?"

I sigh. "It's a long story. There's another a cappella group at our school, and the contest rules state that only one group per organization can enter. So if that group also submits a video, we'll both be disqualified."

"Can't you coordinate with that other group?" Dad asks.

"It's more complicated than that. No one is talking to one another. It's a whole thing."

"Sounds very . . . dramatic," Dad says, just as a deafening "I BEAT YOU!" rings through the window. Dad shakes his head. "Those two. Everything's a competition with them."

"Seems to be the theme of my week." I begin to pull my hair into a ponytail before stopping midway, halted by a new idea. "Wait, that could do it."

"What could do what?"

"We could compete," I say, "for a chance to enter the contest."

Dad scrunches his face, thinking. "Like a sing-off?"

"A sing-off!" I sit up straighter. "Then judges could decide who should represent the school."

"You came up with all that based on their scooter race?"

"Does it make sense?" I ask.

"It seems like a fair way to solve the problem," Dad agrees. "So see? Coming here wasn't a total loss, now, was it?"

I look at him straight-on, relaxed but firm. "I wasn't asking to never come again. I was asking to switch weekends. But you wouldn't hear me out. You never hear me out." I say this last line more quietly.

"'Never' is a big word," Dad says. "I would hope that sometimes, I do. But from now on, I'm going to make it more than 'sometimes.'" When I don't respond, he continues, "Maybe I force things too much. Like I'm afraid if I let you skip one weekend, it will turn into a second, and then a third. And pretty soon, you'll be graduating middle school, and then high school, and I'll barely know you anymore. I want to know you, Wylie."

"But you haven't known me that well for a while," I tell him honestly. "Not since Asher was born, anyway. You didn't even know about Mister Kitters." Dad gives me a questioning look. "Fluffy," I clarify. "Asher's Fluffy. That was my favorite stuffed animal. I brought him everywhere. But I must have left him here one weekend when Asher was a baby, and you didn't realize who he was. So you gave Mister Kitters to Asher. If you had known me well, you would have recognized Mister Kitters."

Dad's face falls, the lines around his mouth growing deeper, and at once, I feel bad. He's trying—truly trying—and I'm still insistent on bringing up the past.

"I know you want to know me," I continue, attempting to smooth things over, "but I don't always feel like myself here. Sometimes it's as if I'm living a double life, like I have to pretend the one at home doesn't exist for two weekends every month."

Dad nods. "I know you may think that I don't, but I do understand how this setup can be hard. As you get older and take part in more activities, I'm sure conflicts are going to come up more often. But I promise to listen so we can work something out. Okay?"

"Okay," I say. "Thank you."

"And I think you're right about coming here. You don't feel as comfortable as we would all like because we don't talk much when you're *not* here. So let's try to keep the lines of communication open—going both ways—so that these weekends feel like less of an obligation for you. When something big happens in your life—you starting your own a cappella group, for instance—I want to hear about it. But I want to hear about the little things too. Your day-to-day things. And same goes for me. It can be through texts, if that's what's easiest. Though you know phone calls are welcome too."

"I like texting. To everyone—not just you—so don't be offended."

"No offense taken," Dad says with a smile. "So would it help if I brought you back to Willow Oak today instead of tomorrow? Do you think your group could still get together?"

"Really? I can text them and ask. Can I see what they say and let you know?"

"Absolutely," Dad says. "Before you leave, though, we need to do one thing: pick a date for the family Christmas card picture. You know Amy isn't going to let that go."

"Let me know the date options, and I'll make it work," I tell him, rising from the couch. "And thank you, by the way. For understanding."

"And you, too," Dad says as I retreat up the stairs. I enter Amelia's room to text The Intermissions, but first, I rustle around in my bag until I find what I'm looking for. I head across the hall and walk over to Asher's dresser, clearing a place between his model airplanes and toy cars. And there, facing Asher's bed, I place Fluffy back in his rightful home.

★24★

Unfortunately, getting *The Intermissions together over* the weekend proves too tough to coordinate at the last minute. Instead, we decide that on Monday I'll ask Mrs. Nicska if she thinks holding a sing-off against The Overtures is plausible. After all, if she says no, then there's no rush to rehearse. But if she says yes? Then we have a chance. A slim chance, but a chance nonetheless.

"If The Overtures are also planning to submit a video, then I do think a sing-off is a good way to resolve the dilemma," she says, studying the school calendar hanging on her board. "There's a Student Council meeting tomorrow in the auditorium—maybe they could judge? I'm not sure we have time to get the entire school involved."

"Mason and Abigail are both on Student Council," I tell her. "I can ask them."

"And I'll check with their advisor," Mrs. Nieska says. "But in the meantime, tell everyone to come prepared to work their puppy tails off at rehearsal today."

"Will do!" I call as I leave. And as I retreat down the hall toward homeroom, I try to ignore the one dreaded word Mrs. Nieska had mentioned: "auditorium."

I have good news and I have bad news, I text Libby.

Good news first, she replies.

Mrs. Nieska thinks the sing-off is a great idea. She suggested we do it at the Student Council meeting tomorrow.

Amazing! We should totally have a leg up with two Council members in our group!

Yes, fingers crossed, I reply.

Then what's the bad news?

The Student Council meetings take place in the auditorium, I write.

And?

I stare at my screen, not believing she's not picking

up on the problem. I can't get on that stage. Not again. Not so soon. Actually, not ever.

Like I said, we'll cross that bridge when we come to it, she answers.

Libby. We are at the bridge. Crossing it is the issue.

You have a whole day to work up to it, she responds. Plus, I'll be there. I won't let you fall off. The bridge OR the stage.

I send back a smiley face, though it doesn't reflect my own worried expression.

"I have an update," I announce when I reach The Intermissions' lunch table. But before I can continue, Mrs. Nieska appears out of nowhere.

"Problem," she announces. "No, I shouldn't say that. Just a . . . a slight hiccup."

"In other words, a problem," Mason whispers to me.

"What is it?" I ask. "We can't do the sing-off?"

"Oh no, we can," Mrs. Nieska says. "It's only . . . well, they changed the date of the Student Council meeting."

"Oh, that's not an issue. I'm going to skip it today to come to rehearsal," Abigail pipes up. "Mason, can't you do the same?"

"Wait, it's today?" I ask. "I thought it was scheduled for tomorrow."

"They moved this month's," Mason says. "Why?"

My face falls. "The sing-off. We were going to do it at the Student Council meeting."

"Which is now *today*?" Libby screeches. The table falls silent.

"There's no way we can do it today," Audrey insists.

"We were barely going to be ready by tomorrow," Libby agrees.

"We don't even know the whole song," I point out.

"Listen, I know it's not ideal," Mrs. Nieska says, "but this is the fairest way to settle the problem."

"The fairest way would have been for Jada to never have formed her group in the first place," Abigail corrects her.

"And they definitely shouldn't be entering the contest," Audrey adds. "She wouldn't even know about it if not for us."

"But she *does* know, and they're planning on submitting a video," Mrs. Nieska says. "Their faculty advisor said they're insistent, even after knowing the disqualification rule."

"Maybe we should let them do it, then," Libby says quietly. "They'll win anyway. They're theatre people. They know how to sing."

"There's no way we'll beat them without another rehearsal," I say sadly. "Maybe we're delaying the inevitable."

"I would hate to let Jada win," Mason says. "But you two might be right. I feel like we're fighting a losing battle."

"Guys, stop." Oliver pounds his palms on the table. "We need to try. What do we have to lose?"

"Um, our dignity?" Audrey asks.

"We can do a shortened version of 'Somebody to Love,'" Oliver continues. "We'll do the beginning, the first verse, and the first chorus. We can handle that, right? Plus, we shouldn't let Jada's group win by default."

"That's true," Abigail says. "At least this way, we put up a fight. And you never know—maybe Student Council will play favorites and vote for their own."

When no one else speaks, I turn to Mrs. Nieska. "What do you think we should do?"

"I think you sing," she says immediately. "You sing like nobody's listening."

I nod and lift my arm. "Raise your hand if you agree we should do the sing-off today. We won't do it unless it's unanimous." Oliver raises his hand first, followed by Abigail, and then Audrey. I look over at Mason, and he waves his hand high. Which leaves only Libby.

"This was your idea," I remind her. "The contest, even the a cappella group itself."

"That part was your idea," she counters.

"Only because you planted the seed in my head."

"I just don't want to be disappointed," Libby says softly, "when we lose."

"There's only one solution to that," Mason tells her. "We don't lose."

Libby smiles. "Easier said than done. But okay—if all of you think we should do it, then I do too." She places her own hand in the air.

"Then it's settled," I announce. "Today, we'll sing like nobody's listening. Because for all we know, nobody will be!"

★25★

But by the time we reach the wings of the stage, the confidence I built up during lunch melts away. The back of my neck is tingly, my hands are cold, my forehead is hot, and my feet feel as heavy as cement-filled balloons.

"I don't think I can do this," I whisper to Libby urgently.

"Sure you can," she says. "Pretend the Student Council members are in their underwear."

"It's not that. It's the stage—the lights. I feel it happening again."

At this, Libby grabs my wrists and looks me squarely in the eye. "Listen to me. That was a million years ago. That stage has nothing over you."

"We're not going on the risers, are we?" I ask. "We never discussed our formation. I can't go on the risers."

"Then we won't go on the risers," Mason pipes up behind me. And while I'm mildly embarrassed he's overheard my freak-out, I'm too relieved at the phrase "won't go on the risers" to care. "You've got this."

I release my wrists from Libby's grasp and shake them out. Then I wiggle my ankles and roll my head, one way and then the other, trying to calm myself. "Here they come," Oliver whispers, and we watch The Overtures walk to the center of the stage, all with large, phony smiles plastered on their faces.

"They look plastic," Audrey murmurs.

"Wait—they have props?!" Abigail squeals, pointing to their top hats and canes. "How did they have time to pull together props?"

"They probably stole them from the musical," Mason guesses. "Just like they stole the a cappella idea from us."

The choral teacher blows a single tone into her pitch pipe, and The Overtures stand up straighter. Then, simultaneously, they lift their canes and begin banging the tips on the stage, once, twice, three times, cueing their own rhythm. Jada steps out in front of the group and sings a single word: "One!"

"Singular sensation," the rest of The Overtures join in.

"They're doing 'One' from *A Chorus Line*," I whisper to Libby.

"Is that a musical?" she asks, and I nod. "Of course." She twirls the end of her braid around her finger as we turn our attention back to the stage. Besides singing—convincingly and in tune—The Overtures perform perfectly rehearsed choreography. They lift their top hats, they move about the stage in coordinated motions, and toward the end, they even form a kick line.

"We might be in trouble," Abigail says, not bothering to lower her voice as The Overtures come to a crescendo.

"Yeah, there's no way we can beat that," Audrey agrees sadly.

"We don't have to beat that," Oliver counters as the Student Council applauds. "We're completely different from them. They're all show, all razzmatazz. We have heart."

"Are we going on the risers?" Abigail asks. "Maybe that will make us look more professional, since we don't have any choreography or props or—"

"No! No risers!" I call out. "I'm begging you."

"I have a different idea," Libby says, and she grabs Oliver with one hand and me with the other. "Mason, take Wylie's hand. Audrey, take Mason's. Abigail, Audrey's." We follow her directions as I hear Mrs. Nieska introducing us. "Now let's go!" Libby calls excitedly, pushing Oliver onto the stage with a jolt. The two of them take off running toward the center, dragging the rest of us behind them like a tail. When we reach the middle, Libby drops my hand and places her right arm around my waist and her left around Oliver's.

"Now hold on to each other," she hisses, and we do so obediently. I close my eyes and reopen them slowly, and the room before me remains steady, the faces of the Student Council members coming into sharper focus. My feet feel solid on the ground, my body stable with the arms of my friends gripping me securely.

Libby nudges me. "See? You can't fall off the stage with us holding on to you." I smile widely, beyond grateful to have her—and the rest of The Intermissions—by my side. We turn to the front and watch for Mrs. Nieska's cue. She leads us in taking a few deep breaths, and then she gives Mason the signal.

"Can anybody find me . . . ," he belts, his voice rising over the crowd and filling the auditorium. The rest of us open our mouths to join him. And though we may not have costumes or dance moves or one bit of polish, we sound strong. We're not the most musical or the most prepared or the most well trained, but we are definitely in sync with one another. We're one unit, six individual voices blending to create a singular sound, unique in its particular melody.

The Intermissions stand opposite The Overtures on stage to wait for the results, the chain of arms encircling our waists still unbroken.

"They have to vote for us, don't they?" Oliver whispers. "Is anyone from their group on Student Council?"

"I'm not optimistic," Abigail says quietly. "If they choose us, they might be afraid that The Overtures will protest on account of favoritism."

"Nothing like a rigged election," Mason says wryly as the eighth-grade president approaches the microphone. The Intermissions seem to inhale as one as Mrs. Nieska gives us an encouraging thumbs-up.

"After careful consideration," the eighth grader begins, "the Student Council of Willow Oak Middle

School has come to a vote. It was a tight race, a hard decision. But ultimately . . ."

"Spit it out already," Audrey mutters.

". . . we've reached the conclusion that the a cappella group who should represent our school in the *Non-Instrumental* contest is . . ." Our grips tighten around one another, tense with anticipation.

". . . The Overtures!"

Jada's group erupts in a chorus of whoops and cheers, and at Mrs. Nieska's insistence, we clap halfheartedly. Without a word, we retreat offstage with Mrs. Nieska, who is insisting that we did a great job. And while I know she means it, I can't help but be bothered that, in the end, it didn't matter. Our hard work didn't pay off. The Overtures won.

Jada won.

I look over to where they're celebrating. Or at least, where five members of The Overtures are celebrating, as Jada stoops off to the side gathering her things. And while her licorice strands are mostly hiding her face, I can tell one thing: Jada looks miserable.

She suddenly lifts her head and catches my eye. For a moment, I expect her to smirk, to gloat about her win, to permanently seal the door closed on our friendship.

But instead, Jada's face remains gloomy as she rises to her feet and crosses the stage in my direction.

"Can we talk?" she asks when she reaches me, and Libby and Mason appear at my side, as if my body-guards. "Alone?" she clarifies. "Please?"

I kind of want to say no, to shut Jada down, to reject her like she abandoned me. But no matter how hard I try to ignore them, Mom's words keep floating through my mind, reminding me not to throw away a friendship over one fight. Not when there's a chance that it can be saved. And so, even though it may be a mistake, I nod.

"Don't leave without me," I tell Libby and Mason. "I'll be right back."

Jada and I walk to the farthest corner of the wings, camouflaged behind the backstage curtains. "This isn't fair," she says as soon as we're by ourselves.

"Huh?" I can't tell if her tone is belligerent or not.

"This. This whole thing. You're the one who started the a cappella group, and found out about the contest—"

"Libby found out about the contest," I correct her.

"But still," Jada says. "This is your thing. You're the one who deserves the call with Colby, and now you don't even get to send in a submission. That's not fair."

I stare at Jada blankly. Is she being serious? She's

talking as if she isn't involved in this problem, as if she didn't go behind my back, as if her group isn't the reason why The Intermissions can't win the contest.

"I know—I know." Jada holds up her hand as if to stop me, even though I haven't spoken yet. "I did this. I get that."

"And . . . ?" I prompt her.

"And I'm sorry. I'm really sorry," Jada says. "And I want to fix it."

"It's too late to fix it," I tell her coolly. "What's done is done."

"Not if you join The Overtures," Jada says.

I widen my eyes. "I would never leave my group." And though I don't say it out loud, what I want to add is, *like you left me*.

"They can all join," Jada says. "We can merge groups."

"There's no way they'll go for that. *I* won't even go for that."

"Wylie, please," Jada begs. "Please let me make it better. Let me talk to them."

I run my hand through my hair, thinking. "And what would The Overtures say about this?"

"They'll agree," Jada says. "They didn't understand

why we were having this sing-off in the first place. They asked why we couldn't just submit one audition tape together. I'm the one who insisted." She looks suddenly sheepish, and I feel my guard lowering ever so slowly.

"I don't know," I tell her. "I feel like if you had truly wanted to make amends, you would have done so before. Now that you won, it's like a pity apology."

"It's not," Jada insists. "I wanted to say something before—a bunch of times. I just . . . I didn't know what to say. This whole argument blew up so much, and so quickly, and I wasn't sure how to repair things. But I'm trying to do so now. Please let me."

I face her silently, thinking about this. "You would need to apologize," I begin, "to the rest of The Intermissions. For the way you acted."

"They weren't nice to me either," Jada says defensively, and I give her a look. "But okay, yes, I'll apologize." Jada and I collect our things and then exit into the hall, where The Intermissions are standing on one side and The Overtures on the other, looking the polar opposite of a united front.

★26★

When I see the wary way *The Intermissions* are looking at Jada and me, I fear I've made a mistake. Is letting her propose this merger a bad decision? Would combining the two groups ever work? Is it worth doing for the sake of the contest? But then again, we only have three days left—how could we get on the same page in so little time? It feels like what Jada is about to ask is impossible.

"What is this about?" Mason whispers to me. "Did she call us over to rub it in?"

"She has an idea," I tell him.

"Whatever it is, the answer—" Mason begins, but Jada cuts him off.

"I'm sorry," she says, facing The Intermissions, and they stare back at her, expressionless.

"For what?" Abigail challenges her, she and Audrey both leaning against the wall with their arms crossed, shielding themselves.

"I've made some mistakes this week," Jada says.

"Understatement of the century," Audrey mumbles.

"You two should understand," Jada says, turning in their direction. "You're best friends, aren't you?" Abigail and Audrey nod tentatively. "I can tell just by looking at you. So you know how it is, how important you are to each other, and how much you can hurt one another." Jada glances in my direction and pauses, as if waiting for a reaction, but no one says anything.

After a beat, Mason asks, "Are you getting to your point?"

Jada takes a deep breath. "But best friends, even when they fight, are still stronger together than they are apart. And the same could be true for our groups. We could join forces. And we could become even better. We could win this contest *together*."

Abigail and Audrey drop their arms to the side,

looking mildly less hostile. "So you expect us to join your group?" Audrey asks.

"It wouldn't be my group," Jada insists. "It wouldn't be anyone's group. It would be all of ours. The Intermission Overtures." I look around, and no one looks entirely convinced. "What do you think?"

Mason leans down. "Is this what you want?" he whispers in my ear.

I think for a moment and then nod. "Okay, then," Mason says, turning back to Jada.

"We should vote," he announces. "Everyone close your eyes, and on the count of three, if you're in favor of joining forces, raise your hand. One . . . two . . . three." I close my eyes and thrust my hand in the air. "Now on three, open your eyes so we can see the results. One . . . two . . ."

And as the hallway comes back into view, I see all twelve of us waving a hand in the air. The Intermission Overtures. Definitely different from how we started, but maybe, hopefully, even stronger than before.

Over dinner that night, I tell Mom about the sing-off and the results and Jada's proposal. "So you and Jada had a talk?" she asks.

"Once the groups merged, we just got down to business," I explain. "We didn't have a huge discussion about it. We had already said what we needed to."

Mom nods. "I'm glad you two worked things out. So the taping is on Thursday?"

"Yes. Which doesn't leave us much time, but we'll do the best we can." I tell her the rest of the details, and once we finish dinner, I find my phone to text Dad. I write to him about the events of the day, and he answers immediately, Thanks for keeping me updated! Please pass along the video when you have it. I'm sure Asher and Amelia would love to see the finished product too.

Will do! I reply as a new text from Jada flashes across my screen.

So I think we should pick a new song, I read. I know this will be more complicated, but it might be the best way to make the group feel like one, rather than "your song" versus "my song." You know what I mean?

I do. But we only have three days left, including Thursday. That's not much time to start from scratch.

But if we go with one of our previous songs, half of us will be starting from scratch anyway, Jada says.

Good point. Okay, let's pick a new one tomorrow at lunch. Can everyone meet at The Intermissions' table?

Maybe we need a new table, too, **Jada begins.** Not The Intermissions' table, not The Overtures' table. Nothing where anyone feels like it's their "turf." Does that make sense?

Yes. How about our old table? If the twelve of us squeeze together, there should be room.

Perfect, **Jada responds.** Did you get everyone's number today? Can you send a group text?

Yeah, I'll do that now. I open a new chain and begin adding numbers, but then I think better of it. Instead, I walk to the door, call, "Be right back!" to Mom on my way out, and scamper across our yard to Libby's.

"Don't tell me—another crisis?" she asks as soon as she answers my knock. "That didn't last long."

"No," I say. "Can I come in for a second?"

"Sure." Libby swings the door wider, and I follow her to the kitchen table and take a seat. "So what's up?"

"I wanted to make sure you were okay with everything that happened today."

"Putting the groups together?" Libby asks, and then she shrugs. "I figure anything that gives us a better chance of winning is good, right?"

"But I didn't want you to feel like you had to say yes," I continue. "Just because Jada and I are friends again, that doesn't mean that I want us to—"

"Wylie." She stops me. "We're good. Promise."

I sit back, relieved. "Would you also be good with the new group eating lunch together tomorrow?" I ask. "I wanted to check with you before texting everyone."

"The more the merrier," Libby says. "But do we have room at our table?"

"There's one in the blue cafeteria where we should fit."

"Cool," Libby says. "We'll probably take up almost the entire thing."

"I know. I've always wondered what it was like to sit at one of those tables, to be a part of a larger group."

"What do you think the other people in the cafeteria will call us?" Libby asks. "Like the theatre people, the brainiacs, the band geeks . . . What will we be?"

"The Intermission Overtures?" I guess.

"Maybe after Colby discovers us, we'll get so famous that we'll have to start auditioning," Libby says. "Wait, never mind, that's a terrible idea."

"Why? Not that I think we should start aud—"

"Because if we make everyone try out, then what are the chances I'd get in again?" Libby asks. "Slim to none!"

I burst out laughing. "I wouldn't worry about that. I'm pretty sure you're here to stay. Do you want to come watch tonight's *Non-Instrumental* in a few?"

"Yes!" Libby exclaims. "I also wouldn't say no to a bag of tortilla chips. Just sayin'."

"You got it," I tell her. "Would you mind if I asked Jada, too? She hasn't seen any of this season yet."

"Sure," Libby answers. "See you soon." I dart outside and back across our lawns, pulsing with anticipation. But for the first time in ages, Colby isn't the one I'm most looking forward to seeing tonight, not with the promise of my two closest friends assembled on either side of me, turning our shared experience into a memory.

★27★

The following afternoon, The Intermission Overtures assemble at Jada's and my old lunch table, squeezing together until one can't tell where The Intermissions end and The Overtures begin. (Though I do notice that Jada makes a point to sit as far away from Mason as possible.)

"So if we're going to make the most of our next two rehearsals, I think we need to decide on a song, and fast," I tell them.

"We're not doing 'Somebody to Love'?" Audrey asks.

"Or 'One'?" a former member of The Overtures pipes up.

"We thought it would be best to start with a fresh slate," Jada says, "so that no one knows the song any better or worse than someone else."

"Why don't we let Mrs. Nieska pick?" Abigail asks. "She chose the song for us last time, and she knows what works best for a cappella groups."

"We could do that," I begin, "but I think we'll make the most of our practice time later if we already know what we want to sing. Or at least if we have ideas to run by her."

"Haven't you seen every episode of *Non-Instrumental*?" Oliver asks Libby. "Any songs stand out?"

Libby drums her fingers against her cheek, thinking. "Metronome Mayhem performed a song on swings, which is my all-time favorite. Remember I showed it to you?" she asks me.

"Yes, that was fantastic," I agree.

"I'll look for it," Jada volunteers, picking up her phone.

"I've never actually seen the show," Audrey reveals. "I meant to watch it last night, and then I forgot."

"Me too," a few others add, and I look around the table, dumbfounded.

"So we're trying to win a contest for a show most of us have never seen?" I ask.

"That should be our group homework tonight," Abigail suggests. "Watch at least one episode—I'm sure most of them are available online."

"They are," Libby confirms. "But if we ever want to do a group viewing party, I have a lot of them saved on my laptop."

"We could do it at my place," Mason pipes up. "We have a huge TV in our den that can be connected to a computer—we should be able to screen the show that way."

I look around to gauge people's reactions, and everyone but Jada seems to like Mason's offer. "That could be fun," I say. "But before we plan anything, I think we need to pick a song . . . and then practice it."

"Boy, such a taskmaster," Mason teases me.

"Found it!" Jada calls out. "The song is 'Lean on Me.'" She flips her phone around so the rest of us can watch.

"So we would need swings . . . ?" Abigail asks.

"No, we don't have to copy them," I say. "I don't

think we should focus on choreography—it would probably be best if we keep it simple."

"The song is pretty," Audrey says, tilting forward to hear. "I think it could work."

"It has a good message, too," Libby says. "About friendship and stuff."

"So what do we think?" I ask. "Are we decided?" Slowly, everyone nods their agreement.

"I think we should sing it as a group, though," Mason states. "No solos or anything."

"No, there should be solos," Jada disagrees, and I brace myself for an argument. But then she continues, "Wylie and Libby should do the solos. You two started this whole thing. You deserve them."

Everyone sits silently for a moment, taking this in, before Libby responds, "That's nice, but no thank you. If we're going to have a chance to win, we need to utilize our strongest voices, which mine is not. Wylie, you and Jada should do the solos. You've been friends forever. It fits the theme of the song."

Jada looks across the table to me, her eyebrows piqued. "What do you think?" she asks.

"I don't think solos will work," I tell her. "But I think a duet could."

* * *

The night before the *Non-Instrumental* deadline, The Intermission Overtures gather in Mason's den, fortifying ourselves for the next day's recording with a group viewing party. I sweep my eyes over the scene, and it makes me grin. After years of wondering what it would be like to have a larger friend group—one with a common purpose and a single goal—I'm now a part of one. And it makes me even happier than I had imagined.

"Daydreaming much?" Mason appears next to me, snapping me back to the present.

"Observing," I tell him. "By the way, is that the infamous seesaw?" I point out the window to the backyard, where a rickety contraption sits on the edge, looking like it hasn't been touched in a decade.

"That's the one," Mason says. "I keep telling my parents we should chop it up for firewood, but they're sentimental about it."

"Brings back fond memories of your first epic battle?"

"Oh, that was far from my first battle," Mason says, a smile unhinging his mouth. "And it was definitely not my last."

"Ha. Yes, as I'm well aware. What's the deal with you and Jada anyway? Why do you insist on torturing each other? Don't you think we're getting a little old for it?"

"Possibly," Mason responds with a shrug. "But I guess it's become a habit. And plus . . . never mind."

"No, no. You can't do that," I tell him. "'Never mind' is the most annoying phrase in the English language."

Mason turns slightly away, crossing his arms and jutting his hip against the wall, uncomfortable.

"What is it?" I ask him, trying to sound lighthearted. "Do you like her or something?"

"No!" Mason answers immediately, as if I've struck him. And then, more quietly, he clarifies, "I don't like Jada. Not like that. I just . . . Jada is always around you. And you're always around Jada. So bothering Jada meant that I had an excuse to be around Jada, which meant . . ." Mason raises his eyes from the floor, meeting mine, begging me to understand.

I feel a faint blush filling my cheeks. Mason Swenson likes me? In all the years I had spent refereeing his fights with Jada, I never would have guessed it. It hadn't even crossed my mind—if anything, I thought he must secretly have a crush on Jada. But me?

"Wow" is all I manage to respond, fully flustered.

"Sorry," Mason begins, "if I made things weird. I just always thought you were interesting. Jada is so dramatic. She has so much to say, and everyone has to hear what she's thinking. You hang back more. But, I don't know, it sounds odd to say it out loud. . . . I was intrigued by you. Is that strange?"

"Yes," I answer him honestly. "I'm really not that interesting."

"Look at this, though," Mason says, gesturing toward the couches. "You pulled this off. Not many people could do that."

"I had help. Lots of it," I say. "*You* helped me."

"It was fun," Mason says. "It *is* fun."

"So does this mean you and Jada can finally call a truce?"

"Not sure that's a good idea," Mason says. "As much as she acts like she's aggravated, I get the impression that she enjoys the attention."

This makes me laugh. "You're probably right. But do me a favor and don't do anything too outrageous. I can't take another breakup of The Intermission Overtures."

"Deal," Mason replies, reaching out his hand to shake mine as the opening chords of the *Non-Instrumental* theme song fill the den.

"It's on!" Libby announces happily. "Mason, can you turn it up?" Mason walks away as my phone vibrates with a new photo text from Dad. Zooming in, I see Asher gripping Mister Kitters—er, Fluffy—around the neck. Wishing you luck at tomorrow's recording! Dad has written beneath it.

"Wylie, get over here!" Jada calls. "We're taking a group portrait." I hurry over and jump into the shot, surrounded by the people I feel lucky to call my own. And as Abigail snaps our photo, I find my grin widening ever further, a smile framed in friendship.

★28★

For our Non-Instrumental *taping, we decide to record in* the place where the twelve of us came together as a group: our newly claimed cafeteria table. We stand around it, trying to figure out the best way to arrange ourselves.

"What if half of us stand on a bench, and the other half on a table?" Mason suggests.

"That's even more terrifying than the risers," I tell him.

"And I don't want to be responsible for any of you

cracking your noses when the table buckles," Mrs. Nieska adds.

"Then how about we sit on the benches?" Libby offers. "Six on one side, six on the other, facing the middle?"

"It might be hard to hear one another that way," Abigail counters.

"Wait, I have an idea," I say, stepping onto a bench and then sitting on the table, my back toward its center. "Now someone else, sit behind me and face the other way."

"It should be Jada," Libby says, "since you two are singing together."

Jada follows my directions, and once she's in the appropriate position, I tell her to lean her back against mine. "Get it? Like 'Lean on Me'? We're giving them a visual."

"Brilliant," Jada says. "Do you think it will work on camera?"

"We can ask my dad when he gets here," Libby says. "But it's a great idea."

"Why don't the rest of you get into place so we can see how it sounds when you sing?" Mrs. Nieska suggests. The remaining ten slide onto the table beside Jada and me, five on one side and five on the other, all back-to-back. As we finish assembling, Libby's dad walks in towing a bag of camera equipment.

"Let's do a run-through while we wait for Mr. Soleil to set up," Mrs. Nieska says. She cues us, and we begin, raising our voices so that they fill the massive space. With this setup, I can't hear Jada during our duet as well as I would like, but I still think we do okay.

And clearly, so does Libby's dad, since he bursts into passionate applause the second the song is over. The twelve of us high-five and congratulate each other, and then we look toward Mrs. Nieska expectantly, waiting for a compliment. Instead, we find her resting her chin in her hand, her brow furrowed and her glasses drooping perilously close to the tip of her nose.

"What's wrong?" I call out as the rest of The Intermission Overtures grow silent.

"I'm just . . . thinking," Mrs. Nieska says.

"We weren't good?" Jada asks.

"You guys were great," Mrs. Nieska says. "But the acoustics might be a problem. Especially with you facing two different directions."

"We don't have to arrange ourselves like this," I say. "If you think we'd be better off—"

"I think it's the room," Mrs. Nieska interrupts. "It's too cavernous in here, and the sound is getting lost. We might be better off on the stage."

My stomach flips at this news, and even though Mason is sitting right beside me, when he speaks, it sounds like he's light-years away, my ears cloudy with worry. "What about the red cafeteria?" he suggests.

"That will be the same problem," Mrs. Nieska says. "Rooms this big absorb sound, like it's swallowed up the second it's released. Let me see if the musical is rehearsing on the stage today. If they're not, that would be a better option." She walks toward the exit, and as everyone else stands, I grab Libby's elbow.

"No risers, right?" I whisper urgently. "Promise me you won't let them go on the risers."

"You'll be fine, whatever it is," Libby tells me. "You know why?"

"Why?"

"Because you've got us to *lean* on," she says, and then she laughs uproariously at her own joke. With that, the nerves fluttering inside me slow their flight ever so slightly. Proof, I suppose, that sometimes, all it takes is one friend to have your back, whether or not they're leaning against it.

* * *

The Intermission Overtures assemble in the wings of the stage as Mrs. Nieska and Mr. Soleil fuss with the camera equipment. I bend my knees over and over, willing myself to hold it together. You did this three days ago, I assure myself. The fear is behind you. You've cured yourself. But my pep talk fails to bring the jitters to a halt.

"Hey." Libby appears next to me. "You won't fall. We won't let you. I promise."

"What's going on?" Jada approaches us, and after taking one look at me, she continues, "Oh no, not this again." She shoves her arm around mine, forming a tight link with my elbow. "You've got this," she asserts, in a tone that makes it impossible to argue. Libby grabs my other arm and fastens herself to my side, gesturing for Oliver to join us. One by one, we line up, attached in a single chain.

"Are you guys ready?" Mrs. Nieska calls from the audience, and I lift my chin high, attempting to bolster myself with newfound bravery.

"We're ready!" I call back, and we tread to the center of the stage, swinging ourselves around until we're facing the front, Jada and me positioned in the middle.

As I look out at the rows of empty seats, the anxiety melts away, squashed by the pressure of my friends' grips clasped around me. On Mrs. Nieska's cue, we begin singing, the words of "Lean on Me" reverberating off the insulated walls.

Lean on me, when you're not strong,

And I'll be your friend. I'll help you carry on.

With Jada on one side and Libby on the other, the meaning behind the lyrics resonates even more strongly. As Jada and I sail through our duet, I have flashbacks of the dozens of songs we've performed as a pair. In what feels like an instant, The Intermission Overtures reach the final measure. And as we belt the last note proudly, I'm awed by how far we've come, deciding that, no matter what happens with the contest, I couldn't be more grateful that it has brought us together.

"Do you have the first two episodes of this season's *Non-Instrumental* saved?" Jada asks as we make our way to Mrs. Nieska's classroom to gather our belongings, our rendition of "Lean on Me" safely preserved on Mr. Soleil's camera.

"Of course," I say. "I couldn't bring myself to delete Colby so soon."

"I'd like to see them," Jada says. "We could even update the scrapbook, if you want. It must be gathering dust."

"Wait a minute." I stop short in the middle of the hall. "I can't believe I forgot to tell you. Remember when Asher and Amelia stayed at my house?" Jada nods. "Amelia decided to use our scrapbook as her personal coloring book. So there are now four-year-old scribbles all over Colby's face." Jada laughs loudly at this, which makes me laugh too. "Maybe it's the universe's way of saying that our Colby days really are behind us. It's like the end of an era."

"Wylie!" Libby screeches, and I whirl around. She runs up to us at full speed, Abigail trailing behind her. "Look, look, look!" Libby thrusts Abigail's phone in my face, the group portrait we took at Mason's house filling the screen.

"Yeah, it's cute," I say. "I'm going to print it out and hang it on my—"

"LOOK WHO LIKED IT!" Libby yells at full volume. I scroll down, where I find Colby's screen name staring back at me.

"No way!" I exclaim, turning the phone toward Jada. "How did he even see it?!"

"When I posted it, I added the hashtag for the *Non-Instrumental* contest," Abigail explains as Audrey joins us. "He must have found it that way."

"Maybe now he'll look for our video!" Libby says. "Come on. We have to show the others." She grabs Abigail's phone from my hand and the three of them take off.

"Well," Jada begins with a chuckle, "so much for the end of an era, huh?"

"It's like Colby's giving us a sign," I agree. "That we shouldn't give up on him yet."

"Looks like you created another fan." Jada points after Libby. "Maybe she's going to want to take over the scrapbook with you. Kick me out of the equation." I can tell that she's trying to say this jokingly, but there's a tinge of concern behind her words.

"No. Colby will always be our thing," I tell her forcefully. "You, me, and Libby, we can find our own thing. As a trio." Jada doesn't say anything, and I'm momentarily afraid this is going to lead to another argument, and so soon after we've reconciled.

But after a second, she responds, "That sounds good," and I smile at her appreciatively. "But now I have a request for you," she continues. "While we're being inclusive, can we draw a line when it comes to Mason?

I don't want to have to deal with him any more than necessary."

The corners of my mouth creep up into a smirk, recalling Mason's and my conversation from last night. "I won't invite him to join us without telling you," I assure her. "But I can't promise that we won't hang out with him someday. I swear he's not so bad. He's kind of nice."

"Yeah, right. I think all of this a cappella is starting to scramble your brain cells, Wy," Jada teases me, throwing her arm around my shoulders as we enter Mrs. Nieska's classroom, where we find the rest of The Intermission Overtures milling around, chattering about Abigail's photo.

And as thankful as I am to have Jada back, I can't help but think that if it hadn't been for our fight, this brand-new group of friends may never have existed. So maybe Mom was right—that even in the closest friendships, it's valuable, every once in a while, to step away from your best friend's side in order to discover what you can conquer by yourself. To find your own voice before blending it back together again, this time in perfect harmony.

ACKNOWLEDGMENTS

A crescendo of thanks to Alyson Heller, who never fails to find the narrative melody.

A vibrato of appreciation to Charlie Olsen, who constantly knows how to bring out the harmony.

And a round of applause to Mara Anastas, Fiona Simpson, Faye Bi, Elizabeth Mims, Jessica Handelman, Cat Hayden, and the rest of the Aladdin team, for always managing to make a book SING!

If you loved Sing Like Nobody's Listening,
read on for a peek at

SPRING Break MISTAKE

Allison Gutknecht

The worst thing about my sister is her smile.

It's not that it's a bad smile—it's a great smile, actually. One of the best there is. It's the kind of smile that seems ever-present, even when Arden is scowling. I would think the expression "she can light up a room" was a load of baloney, if it weren't for Arden's sparkle of a mouth. And the worst part is she didn't even do anything to deserve it—not really, anyway. She was gifted with picket fence–straight teeth, with a coat of white shine to match.

I, however, have the kind of teeth that require four years of braces just for the mere hope that they might someday end up not being an abject disaster. This is the injustice of my life.

Arden is flashing one of her signature smiles toward me at the moment, all while lounging on my window seat with her feet propped up on the grids of the glass pane.

Which she knows I hate.

"Get your hooves off my window," I tell her, scrolling absentmindedly through the PhotoReady app on my phone. "You're smudging my view."

"I'd hardly call this a view," Arden argues. "A bunch of trees and a rusty old swing set." I click out of PhotoReady and open the camera, aiming it in Arden's direction.

"Say cheese," I coo in a singsong voice. I pretend to snap a picture as Arden turns her head in my direction. Her feet fly off the window as she scrambles to stand.

"Don't you dare post that." She leaps across the room and flops onto the bed next to me. I roll in the opposite direction until my feet hit the floor, phone still in my hand, then I walk to the window and make a great display of lifting one of the throw pillows to clean her toe print off the glass. But at the last second, I snap a photo of it instead.

"Um, what are you doing?" Arden asks.

"Taking a picture of the mark your man-toes made,"
I say. "It could probably be studied in the Museum of
Natural History."

Arden crosses her arms and stomps her foot against
my bedspread. "Delete the photo," she tells me in her
best principal voice. "Now."

"Oh, calm down," I tell her, settling onto the window seat and texting the toe-print shot to my best
friend, Celia, with the caption, *For your heart collection*,
before quickly deleting it.

"Prove you erased it," Arden says, reaching for my
phone. I toss it on the bed beside her and watch her
examine my albums. Satisfied, she slides it away from
her. "Here's a rule for Florida—only take good pictures
of me." I snort. "Or better yet, don't take pictures of me
at all. That's the only way I'll know I'm safe. I mean,
the worst pictures of me ever taken are the ones from
spring break." Arden pulls at the ends of her thick,
dark curls, twirling one around her finger. It is true that
every single year, the second Arden steps off the plane
and into the Florida humidity, her hair frizzes up like
a beehive. What is *not* true is that this frizz results in
bad pictures of her—maybe slightly worse than usual,
but still not bad.

After all, she has that smile.

In contrast to Arden's mane, my hair only seems to grow limper in the Florida heat. Really, between our teeth and our hair, no one would ever believe Arden and I were sisters. As wild and unruly as Arden's hair is, mine is equally as fine and straight. "Strawberry blond" is what everyone calls it, though in the wrong light, it tends to look baby pink, like the color of a newborn girl's nursery.

And for some reason, the Florida sun is definitely the "wrong light" for my hair.

"Well, I'm sure the Backgammon Bandits and the Pinochle Posse won't mind me taking *their* pictures," I say.

Arden sighs. "What's the point of living in Florida if you don't live on the beach?" she asks. "Or at least *near* a beach."

"Or near Disney World," I add. "I'd settle for Disney World." Our grandparents have managed to pick the only place in Florida that is far from a beach, far from Disney World, and far from anything but their own retirement community. When Arden and I were little, the place seemed like a giant adventure. Our grandparents' home became our private village for the week, complete with

Suddenly anxious, my fingers seem to move in slow motion as I open the body of the e-mail:

Dear Avalon Kelly,

Congratulations! You have been selected to take part in this year's junior high PhotoReady retreat (the "PhotoRetreat") in New York City!

My eyes only land on every third word as I read, the entire e-mail beginning to swim together into a gigantic blur. I start pacing the floor in a semicircle, around my bed, from one wall to the other, and then back. I hold my phone in front of me, hoping that with every lap, I'll be better able to concentrate on its contents, but I only seem to grow more nervous.

Celia and I had applied to this PhotoRetreat—a one-week getaway to New York for seventh- and eighth-grade PhotoReady users—a few months ago. For consideration, you had to use the app to create your own photo project, which is how #CeliaHeartsNYC came to be. Celia had made it her mission to photograph hearts she found "in the wild"—those created by the cream in our science teacher's coffee, or by two perfectly folded book pages, or in the snow or with sidewalk chalk, or from a bent toilet paper roll. Celia was determined for us to both get accepted into the PhotoRetreat, because "how pools and tennis courts and mysterious games like croquet and shuffleboard. But after twelve years of this annual spring break trip, I had had about all I could handle of backgammon and pinochle.

I walk across the room to retrieve my phone, and then I open PhotoReady again. At the very top of my feed is Arden's toe print—Celia has posted it with the label #CeliaHeartsNYC, courtesy of @AvalonByTheC. I smirk, more grateful than ever that Arden doesn't have a PhotoReady account. I'm sure she wouldn't be pleased to know that her enormous feet marks got a featured mention in Celia's photography project.

"What're you smiling at?" Arden asks.

"Celia's comment on my picture of Jelly," I lie.

Arden rolls her eyes. "You two and your dumb cat photos . . . ," she says, sliding herself off my bed. "I'll leave you alone to be weird by yourself." I climb onto my mattress the second Arden is gone, lying on my back with my knees bent. I hold my phone over my face, flipping through people's pictures. Without Arden, my room is so quiet that when my phone dings with a new e-mail, I nearly drop it on my nose.

I sit up to open my inbox, and three words catch my eye instantly: *Congratulations from PhotoReady!*

much fun would it be to spend a week in New York City *together*?" And while the retreat sounded exciting in theory, in practice, the whole thing made me uneasy. A week away from home, in a new city, with new people, and completely foreign routines? As much as I loved PhotoReady, did I really love it enough to justify five full days away from my comfort zone?

When Celia and I were both wait-listed a few weeks ago, part of me had been relieved. After all, Celia couldn't say I hadn't tried—I had created my own photo project just like she had. Mine was called #IfYouJustSmile, and I had taken close-ups of different parts of my face and then posted two pictures side by side: one where I hadn't been smiling, and another where I had. It showed the squint of my eyes, the crinkles along the sides of my nose, the indentations around my mouth, all of which formed the second I smiled. But in the pictures, I had never actually shown my mouth. Because we already know the problem there.

I sit down on the window seat, tapping my fingernails against the back of my phone. Arden is right—this view isn't exciting. It's sweet, but it's not exciting. The views in New York City would be exciting. The pictures I could take in New York? They would be amazing. It would be a huge opportunity. It would be something I'd be stupid to turn down, to ignore, to delete the e-mail.

It could be fun.

It could be fun, at least, if Celia were there too.

I moan out loud to myself, taking my phone out from under my legs and opening the camera. Aiming the lens out the window, to the same backyard I've seen nearly every day of my life, I center the abandoned swing set and snap a picture. I then open PhotoReady, load the shot into a frame, choose the black-and-white filter, and type a caption: *Old view*.

And as I watch the photo load onto my screen, I wonder if I'm ready to start looking at something new.

I march across the hall to Arden's room and head directly to her wicker rocking chair. Collapsing into it, I announce, "I need to tell you something."

Arden rotates around to face me, a questioning look in her arched eyebrows.

"Wait a second," I begin, dropping my phone on the rocking chair to go shut her door.

"This sounds serious," Arden says.

"It is."

"Did Jelly side-swipe a vase again? Mom can't keep claiming that every vase is her favorite. This is getting ridic—"

"Not about Jelly. About me," I say, returning to the rocker.

"Go on," Arden says, crossing her arms against her chest and leaning back in her seat. Arden is a year younger than me, but we've always acted more like twins—twins who look nothing alike, but twins nonetheless. As if I'm only three minutes older than her, instead of thirteen months. She is mostly my best friend, even more than Celia is—which means she can also drive me battier than anyone else in the world.

But for times like these, she's exactly who I need.

"So . . . ," I begin. "I told you how Celia and I applied for that PhotoReady retreat a few months ago? The one they're doing in New York the week of our spring break?"

"Weren't you wait-listed? Which you decided was their nice way of rejecting you?"

"Yes," I say. "Only we were *actually* wait-listed. And now, I'm . . . not wait-listed."

Arden's eyes widen. "You got in?"

I nod my head slowly. "They just sent me an e-mail."

"No way!" Arden shouts, leaping up from her chair.

"Shhhh." I shush her. "I don't want Mom or Dad to hear."

"Why? That's awesome! I guess you're more talented with that silly camera than I give you credit for." She says this last part with a smirk.

"I'm not sure I'm going to go," I confess.

"Why? A whole week in New York with your camera? Sounds right up your alley."

"Maybe if Celia were going," I say. "But I haven't heard from her, which makes me think she didn't get an e-mail. And I would never go to New York by myself."

Arden stares at me blankly, as if I'm speaking a foreign language. "Um, you have to go. This is, like, a big deal."

"No, I'm not going," I say matter-of-factly. "Unless Celia ends up going too, but otherwise, no way." The skin on my arms begins crawling with goose bumps at the thought of spending a week with a bunch of strangers, away from everything—and everyone—I know.

"Seriously? We were just complaining about having to spend another spring break at the Retirement Ranch. This is your chance to finally do something different."

"You'd want to suffer alone with the Pinochle Posse?" I ask.

"Of course not," Arden answers. "But that doesn't mean you shouldn't go to New York."

It's my turn to be surprised. "That's awfully generous of you," I tell her.

"Oh yes, that's my middle name: Generosity," Arden retorts. "Arden Generosity Kelly."

"Okay, you're no help to me." I stand up to leave, but Arden blocks my path.

"You have to do it," she says in her most serious voice. "You love taking pictures. You love New York."

"We've only been there twice," I point out.

"Yes, and both were over the holiday break," Arden says. "You know what they say—if you can love New York during tourist season, you can love it anytime."

"Who says that?"

"Everyone. Now promise me you'll go. Whether Celia does or not. You will go."

"I can't promise that," I say. "What am I supposed to do—sneak off to New York and hope Celia shows up too? I can't go without her, but I also can't ask her if she got in."

"But you can tell her that *you* did," Arden says. "Let me see that e-mail." I hand her my phone with the letter displayed across the screen.

"'Dear Avalon Kelly,'" Arden reads out loud. "Sounds so official."

"Please don't read it to me," I beg, and Arden scans the rest in silence before fiddling with my phone. When she gives it back to me, Celia's face is on the screen—the picture that pops up whenever I call her, or she calls me.

"Here," Arden says. "Talk to her. She's your best friend. She should be happy for you." Before I can protest, I hear a faint "Hello?" coming from the phone. Celia's voice. I mouth a silent *I hate you* to Arden before darting out of her room and back to my own.

"Hello?" Celia repeats.

"Hey, sorry," I say, shutting the door behind me. "I was running out of Arden's room."

"No problem," Celia says. "What's up?"

I think about how to answer. I suppose Arden is right—I can't keep this news from Celia forever. Especially not now that I've told Arden, who is *never* going to let me keep it a secret.

"So I got an e-mail," I begin.

"Mmm-hmm," Celia says, sounding distracted.

"From PhotoReady," I continue.

"Oh, yeah?" Celia asks, a little more interested.

"About the retreat. Did . . . did you get one?"

"No," Celia answers. "What about the retreat?"

I sit on my bed stiffly, as if bracing for impact. "I got in."

There are a few seconds of silence on the other end of the phone, and then a few more. The quiet goes on for so long that I'm convinced the connection must have failed.

"Celia?" I finally ask.

"I'm here," she says. "Wow. That's . . . great."

"But listen . . ." I begin talking quickly. "You should totally be the one to go—*you're* the one who found out about the retreat. I'll tell them I want to transfer my invitation to you."

"No." Celia stops me. "You can't do that. It said all over the application that invitations were nontransferable."

"Oh," I say. "Then I'll decline it, and maybe they'll let you in instead. Maybe they only want one person per town, so if I say I'm not going—"

"You don't have to do that," Celia interrupts me. "You should go if you want to."

"But I don't, not without you," I tell her. "Promise."

"You shouldn't give up your spot. That would be a waste."

"Well, maybe you'll still get in." I try to say this hopefully.

"Maybe," Celia says, sounding about as confident as I do.

"And if you do, we can still go together," I say. "You know, if our parents agree and everything. But if you don't, I won't go either. I don't even want to go—it wouldn't be fun without you."

"'Kay," Celia says absentmindedly. "Listen, I've got to have dinner. I'll talk to—"

"I'm not going on the retreat," I insist before she can hang up. "I'm going to write back and say *no, thank you*. Plus, it's next week—it's not like they gave me much warning. I already have plans."

"Don't do that. Not yet," Celia says. "Going to your grandparents' lame retirement home doesn't count as 'plans.' No offense. And like you said, maybe I'll still get in. And then we really can go together. Give it a few more days."

"But I don't even want to go," I say.

"You're *scared* to go," Celia tells me. "But I think you *want* to. That's different. Hey, now I really do have to hang up. Just please don't say no yet. Let's see what happens." The line goes silent.

I toss my phone onto the pillow next to me and trace the pattern on my bedspread with the tip of my finger. I had thought keeping the news to myself would be harder than sharing it, but now, the more people that find out, the more nervous I feel.

And the more I wish I had never applied to the PhotoRetreat in the first place.

ABOUT THE AUTHOR

Allison Gutknecht is the author of *Spring Break Mistake,*
The Bling Queen, and the Mandy Berr series, beginning
with *Don't Wear Polka-Dot Underwear with White Pants*
(And Other Lessons I've Learned). After graduating from
the University of Pennsylvania, she earned her master's
degree in Children's Media and Literature from NYU.
Allison grew up in Voorhees, New Jersey, and now lives
in New York City with her rambunctious toy poodle,
Gypsy, and her literate cat, Folly.